THE BODY CHECKER

CATHRYN FOX

COPYRIGHT

Copyright 2018 by Cathryn Fox
Published by Cathryn Fox

ALL RIGHTS RESERVED. Without limiting the rights under copyright reserved above, no part of this publication may be reproduced, stored in or introduced into a retrieval system, or transmitted, in any form, or by any means (electronic, mechanical, photocopying, recording, or otherwise) without the prior written permission of both the copyright owner and the above publisher of this book.

This is a work of fiction. Names, characters, places, brands, media, and incidents are either the product of the author's imagination or are used fictitiously. The author acknowledges the trademarked status and trademark owners of various products referenced in this work of fiction, which have been used without permission. The publication/use of these trademarks is not authorized, associated with, or sponsored by the trademark owners.

This e-book is licensed for your personal enjoyment only.

This e-book may not be re-sold or given away to other people. If you would like to share this book with another person, please purchase an additional copy for each recipient. If you're reading this book and did not purchase it, or it was not purchased for your use only, then please return to your favorite e-book retailer and purchase your own copy. Thank you for respecting the hard work of this author.

Discover other titles by Cathryn Fox at www.cathrynfox.com. Please sign up for Cathryn's Newsletter for freebies, ebooks, news and contests:
https://app.mailerlite.com/webforms/landing/c1f8n1
ISBN 978-1-928056-91-1
ISBN Print 978-1-928056-90-4

JONAH

A loud thump from one of the many upstairs bedrooms pulls me awake. I shift on the sofa, open one eye, and groan. Partly because my place is a disaster after last night's—all night—party, and partly because I have a killer fucking headache that's blurring my vision.

I turn over, using slow, easy movements, and the beer bottles lined up on the coffee table sway as I try to blink the room into focus. I steal a glance at the massive clock on my wall, each tick of the second hand amplified in my head as I discover it's just past noon. Christ, I've only been asleep for a few hours.

I close my eyes as I think about finding my way to my comfortable king-size bed, but another loud thump sets off a pounding behind my eyes. I'm going to fucking kill whoever is stomping around upstairs. But when the noise continues, I realize the banging isn't coming from one of the bedrooms, it's coming from my front door.

I drag my hands through my mussed hair, smoothing it down, and swallow against a dry throat as I try to pull myself together.

Who the hell would be at my door this early on a Saturday morning? All my buddies are asleep in my house. Most have flown back to Boston, my hometown and the spot where I'll be hanging out after a successful season, to celebrate my massive contract extension with the Seattle Shooters, and anyone who knows me, knows I like to sleep in when I'm not on the road.

The knocking continues. "Okay, I'm coming," I yell, and reluctantly climb from the sofa. I grumble under my breath, trip over a pizza box, and stumble to the door. "What?" I asks as I open it, the noon-hour sun burning the shit out of my eyes. I shade my face with my hand, take in the woman on my stoop.

"Jonah," Shari says, and holds a small pink bundle out to me. A small pink bundle that looks as bad-tempered as I feel.

"What's going on?" I ask, as the baby in Shari's arms lets out a loud shriek. Jesus. I falter backward, my head ready to explode from the godawful noise.

"What's going on is I'm tired, Jonah. I haven't slept in four months, and now it's your turn to take care of her."

I squint and look into the baby's blue eyes, take in her tear-streaked cheeks. "What are you talking about?"

"Meet Daisy," she says and shoves the baby into my arms. She cries louder, and I'm sure my head just cracked at the base of my skull.

"Daisy?" I say.

"Yeah, Daisy. Your daughter."

My head rears back. Oh, fuck no. I must be hearing her wrong. Has to be the hangover messing with my ability to comprehend. I pinch my eyes shut and open them again, hoping I'm hallucinating, but nope—Shari and the baby are still there. "What did you just say?"

"Meet Daisy. She's your daughter." Shari pulls a big bag from her shoulders and drops it in front of my bare feet. "You have enough formula and diapers for a couple days. I suggest you do some shopping."

She turns to leave, and I reach out and cup her elbow. "Oh no, no way is this child mine." I try to hand the squirming bundle back, but Shari folds her arms and steps backward, out of my reach.

"Oh, she's yours, all right."

I rack my brain, Think back to the last time Shari was in my bed. "We used protection. I always use protection," I remind her. "You're making a mistake. This kid can't be mine."

"She can and she is." She gives me a look that suggests I'm dense. "The condom broke, remember?"

Wait, was that with Shari?

"No, I don't remember." Okay, I've been with a few girls—or a lot—but I don't remember a condom breaking when I was with Shari. But it's possible it could have. Judging from the bundle in my arms, I'd say it's more than possible. Still, I'm not ready to accept it as truth. I give a hard shake of my head and the room spins around me. "You've got to be mistaken."

"She's four months old, Jonah. A little over a year ago, I was in your hotel room in Philly, and the condom broke."

I remember Philly. Shari had flown there, and we had one hell of a wild weekend, but no way am I ready for a baby, to be a father, which is why I always wear protection.

"Wait, didn't you say you were on the pill?" If I'm remembering correctly, she told me not to bother with the condom, but I used one anyway.

"So you remember that, but you don't remember the condom breaking?"

I search for clarity. Stupid fucking hangover. "I don't know what I remember. But what I *do* know is, you can't leave her here with me," I say, and hold the baby out to her. "I don't know the first things about babies."

"Then you'd better read a book, or google it." Before I can stop her, Shari races down the front steps and hops into her car. The doors slams and without so much as a glance our way, she drives off.

I stand there, the baby still in my outstretched arms as I glance up and down the street.

What the fuck just happened?

Mrs. Johnson, my next door neighbor, leisurely strolls down her driveway, and when her head angles my way, I step back and shut the door. Shit. Shit. Shit. Now what the hell am I supposed to do?

The baby's lower lip trembles as she stares up at me, no doubt as terrified as I am.

"Hey," I say, because I'm an idiot and have no idea how to talk to a baby. She wails again, and I cradle her in my arms the best I can and pick up the bag. I walk to the sofa, sit down and rifle through it. I find a pacifier, and put it in Daisy's mouth, and for all of one second she's satisfied. But before I can pat myself on the back for a job well done, she spits it out and cries some more.

Fuck me!

Panicked, my gaze lands on my cell phone. I pick it up and do a quick search.

What to do when a four-month-old cries.

Okay, shit, she's hungry, and I have to warm her bottle and test it on my arm to ensure it's room temperature. I find a bottle in the bag and hurry to the kitchen to warm it. Since I'm smart enough to know rubber can't go in the microwave, I unscrew the top and place the bottle inside, nuking it for ten seconds. I bounce Daisy gently, trying to console her as I wait for the microwave to beep.

"What the hell, man?" my best friend Zander says from the doorway.

I turn to him, and I must have panic written all over my face, because his eyes go wide and he hurries across the room, coming to my rescue. Zander has a younger sister, took care of he growing up. Surely to God, he'll know what to do with Daisy.

"Dude, what the fuck?" he asks as he takes the wailing baby from my arms. The microwave beeps and I grab her bottle. I screw the top back on, shake it, and test it on my arm. I have no fucking idea if it's too hot or not.

Zander holds his arm out, and I squeeze a few drops for him to test.

"It's fine," he says, and puts the bottle into Daisy's mouth. Her tears stop instantly, and she gobbles the milk. "You want to explain what's going on here?"

I hold my pounding head and gesture toward the living room, needing to sit before I do a face plant. Zander follows me in. He takes the sofa and I take the chair across from him.

"Shari stopped by," I begin, and Zander nods. He knows who I'm talking about. Shari is a puck bunny, and has slept with almost every guy on our team.

He quirks a brow. "And?"

"And she said the baby is mine." I shake my head, refusing to believe it, or to entertain the idea for one second longer.

"Oh man," he whispers under his breath.

"How did this even happen...?"

"Dude, if you don't know that," he teases.

"She can't be mine, Zander. I always use protection."

"Protection doesn't always work, and sometimes condoms break."

"Yeah, she said mine broke, but I don't remember. Then again, we all got pretty fucked up after kicking Philly's ass."

He nods and goes quiet, the way he always does when he's

puzzling something out. "The condom must have broken, Jonah. I can't imagine Shari would lie about something like that?"

I plant my elbows on my knees and rest my forehead in my hands as my heart beats triple time against my ribs. "Yeah, I guess." Little hungry gulping sounds fill the silence, and the pounding in my head subsides slightly. I look at the baby.

Am I really her father?

"I'm not equipped to take care of a child," I say. Jesus, I was an only child growing up, and pretty much catered to by a doting mom. I'm a little embarrassed to admit that I've never had to care about anyone or anything but myself, and I'd call my mother to help right now but she and Dad are away on holiday for the next couple weeks.

"No, but I know who *is* equipped," Zander says.

I lift my head to find Zander feeding the baby with one hand and digging his phone from his back pocket with the other.

"Who?" I ask.

"Quinn."

The invisible belt squeezing my chest eases, and I nod. As a daycare teacher, Zander's younger sister might be equipped to help, but that doesn't mean she will. She doesn't even like me. Why would she step up to the plate to help out?

I listen to the one-sided conversation, and when Zander ends the call, I hold my breath, praying the news is good.

"She's on her way."

Air rushes from my lungs. "Thank fuck."

"Hey, watch your language in front of the child."

"Shit, right."

Zander glares at me, until footsteps on the stairs catch our attention.

"Zander?" Liz asks hesitantly as her gaze moves around the room, settling on the little pink bundle in his arms.

"She's not mine," he says to the only girl he's ever been serious about. "She's Jonah's."

"You're kidding me." She plunks herself down beside Zander. "I had no idea you had a daughter, Jonah."

"That makes two of us," I say.

Liz gathers her hair and pulls an elastic from her wrist to tie it up. "Who's the mother?" she asks.

I open my mouth but Zander answers for me. "Shari," he says. He takes the bottle from the baby's mouth and puts her over his shoulder. Jesus, he's a natural with her. Then again, his mother left when he was young, leaving her two children behind. Quinn was just an infant herself, and at four years old, Zander had to take on a lot of responsibility. I'm sure feeding his baby sister was one of them.

"Watch and learn, Jonah." He taps the baby's back, Daisy lets out a loud burb. Christ, she could put a locker room full of hockey players to shame. Zander chuckles.

"Does she have a name?" Liz asks.

"Daisy," I say, and Liz makes an aww sound.

She touches the baby's little hand. "That's so pretty." She looks at the baby, then at me. "She kind of looks like you, Jonah."

"She looks like Winston Churchill," Zander says, and Liz slaps him.

"That's awful. She's beautiful."

Zander cradles her in his arms again, and now that she has a full belly, she falls asleep.

I look at the bundle all wrapped up in a pink blanket. No way. Now way can I do this. I try to breathe through a fresh burst of panic. But now suddenly I can't seem to fill my lungs.

"She needs a crib," Zander says.

A crib? Sure, like I have one of those just laying around.

"Can I hold her for a bit?" Liz asks. Zander hands the

baby over, and I root through the bag again, to see what supplies Shari left for me.

"You're not going to find a crib in there," Zander ribs, a crooked grin on his face.

"Funny," I say, in no mood for his humor. I find a few more bottles, a stack of diapers and a couple changes of clothes. What the hell do I do when I run out?

Hopefully Shari will come to her senses by then, and come back and rescue her child. What kind of mother just leaves her baby with a guy who has no clue how to take care of her anyway? Then again do, I even want her to come back after a stunt like that?

Daisy makes a cooing sound as Liz snuggles her, and while I'm terrified of the little bundle, it scares me more to think Shari could have just left her somewhere alone, no one to take care of her. An uneasy shiver moves through me, and as I feel a strange protective tug, Zander points to the bottles.

"You'd better put them in the fridge."

"Yeah." I gather up the bottles and the cans of formula. Needing a moment to myself, to wrap my brain around this turn of events, I hurry to the kitchen and open the fridge. I shake my head when I find nothing but beer and wine. A baby can't live on takeout. Wait, does a four-month-old even eat solid food?

Christ, I am so fucked.

My doorbells rings and I head back to the living room to find Zander opening the door for his sister. Her hair in a frazzled mess, she steps around him, plants her hands on her hips and gives me a scalding glare.

Air leaves my lungs in a rush, like I'd just been body checked. For a tiny might of a girl, her scowl sure packs a punch

She waves her finger at me, her mess of short blonde hair bobbing around her chin. "First things first, if you're going to have a baby in here, you need to get this place cleaned up," she says. I take in the room from her eyes. Empty pizza boxes, Chinese food containers, bags of chips and dozens of bottles are littered throughout the room. Yeah, okay, it's a pigsty, but we were celebrating.

"I'm not even convinced she's mine, Quinn."

The amber flecks in her blue eyes flare bright. Could she hate me any more? "Clean up," she says, "and put a damn shirt on already." She starts stacking bottles in her arm, clinking them together, and Zander reaches for the pizza boxes to help.

I stand there, dumfounded. Wait, Quinn is going at this situation like I'm actually going to keep the child here with me, in my house.

Oh, hell no. I'm not fit to be a father.

"I can't keep Daisy here, Quinn," I say, pointing to the sleeping baby in Liz's arms. "I have no idea how to take care of a baby." I grip my hair. "Jesus, I have a career to think about, and the last thing I want is to be a father or settle down with a family."

She glares at me, and so help me God, if looks could kill, I'd be riding shotgun on the bus to Hell.

"It's too late for that now, isn't it?" she says.

Jesus, does she have to be so mean? Yeah, okay, I know I'm a selfish prick, but at least I know it and don't pretend otherwise. And yeah, she's right. It *is* too late for that.

2

QUINN

I'm so pissed off, I'm sure there is steam coming out of my ears. I can't stand for a man to shirk his responsibilities, and seeing Jonah standing there, denying the baby is even his, makes me want to throat punch him.

I've never, for one minute, liked the way my brother or his best friend lived, puck bunnies in their beds every night. At least now Zander has seemed to settle down with Liz. Seriously though, did Jonah not think that it would catch up to him? That something like this would eventually happen? Sure, he's the golden boy of the NHL, but this is reality, and he needs to clean up his act and stand up to be the man Daisy needs him to be. She deserves that much from him. Especially after being abandoned by her mother.

My stomach takes that moment to clench, and I stop what I'm doing long enough to swallow down the pain of my own abandonment. How can a mother just up and leave her child? I glance at the sweet bundle being held by Liz and my heart squeezes.

Jonah must know what I'm thinking because he puts his big hand on my back.

"Quinn, I really appreciate you helping me out like this."

He splays his fingers, and as the heat of his touch goes right through me, goose bumps pebble my skin, despite the warmth inside his mansion.

Honest to God, I hate myself right now. Hate how much I like his touch. He's a selfish prick who cares about no one but himself. How could I ever like a guy like that...fantasize about being in his bed?

I'm such an idiot.

I shake him off me and stiffen. "Let's get one thing straight, Jonah. I'm not here for you, I'm here for Daisy. That poor child can't be left alone with you until you get yourself together and be the father she needs you to be."

He holds his hands up in surrender and steps back. "Okay, thanks for helping, Daisy," he says.

My gaze drops to his bare chest, to the hills and valleys my fingers itch to touch. I briefly pinch my eyes shut and before I can stop myself, I blurt out, "Put on a shirt."

"Okay, okay," he says and darts up his stair. I watch him go, admire his ass in those nice-fitting jeans.

When I look at Liz, she's biting back a smile.

"What?" I ask, and narrow my gaze.

She shakes her head hard. "Nothing."

"That's what I thought."

I carry the empty bottles into the kitchen, and my brother is pulling a garbage bag out from under the sink. "Zander," I say, and he turns to me, a worried look on his face. I drop the bottles into the bag and glance around the kitchen.

"You okay?" he asks

I push crumbs off a chair and drop into it. "Not really."

He sits next to me and puts his hand on my knee. "Sucks for Daisy, huh?"

"Poor little girl." I fight back tears, thinking of my own

childhood. At least I had Zander. He was my best friend growing up. It was always us against the world. He took such great care of me, and still tries to. Often, I have to remind him I'm a grown woman now, but I get his sense of duty to me. It couldn't have been easy for him to step into the role of mother at the tender age of four. Dad was never too right in the head after Mom left, working odd jobs to put food on the table. Most times it was just cereal. I guess he did the best he could at the time. Now we're the ones taking care of *him*. Smoking finally caught up to him, and he's battling lung cancer.

"He'll do the right thing, Quinn. He's a good guy. This just caught him off guard. I probably would have reacted the same way."

I blink up at my brother. "Do you think the baby is his?"

"Shari said it was. Why would she lie about something like that?"

"She sleeps around, Zander. It could be anyone's child."

"I know, but she said the condom broke when she was with Jonah, and the timing is right." My brother goes quiet for a second and looks down, like that thought disturbs him. Like he might have had a broken condom a time or two. Is it possible that he has kids out there that he doesn't know about?

"He's going to need a nanny to help out. He can't bring a baby to Seattle when you guys return for training, or take her on the road with him when you travel," I say, understanding hockey is Jonah's life. He might be a selfish prick, but I'd never want to see him kept from playing the game he loves— the only real thing he loves. I personally know how hard both he and my brother worked to get to where they are now. Talent is one thing, but the passion they both have, the drive, the hours they spend training, that's something else altogether, something admirable.

"Yeah. I know," Zander says. "Do you know any good ones?"

"Unfortunately, no. I can put out some feelers at the daycare and help him interview, though. I want to make sure Daisy gets the best."

"Interview for what?"

We both look up to see Jonah standing in the doorway.

"A nanny," I say, and he opens his mouth like he's going to shoot down the idea. Likely because he still can't accept that the baby is his. I glare at him, and his lips pinch tight. "It will take time to find the right person. Weeks maybe."

Jonah rakes his hands through his mussed hair. "Shit." Dark brown eyes lock on mine, and I brace myself because I know what's coming next. "Quinn, do you think you can stay the night to help me?"

"Well, I'm certainly not going to leave Daisy alone. Poor little girl has been traumatized enough."

"Thanks," he says, and Zander squeezes my knee.

I turn back to him. "Go easy on him, Quinn," he says, loud enough for Jonah to hear. "He's terrified."

I angle my head, let my gaze roam over Jonah's face, his tense posture.

Jesus, Zander is right.

Since the two guys met on the playground back in elementary school, they've pretty much been inseparable. I've seen a lot of emotions cross that man's face, and fear was never one of them. It's clear he's desperate for my help.

As a nurturer by nature, something inside me softens.

I stand. "Okay, I'll stay for as long as you need me to. We'll start a search for a nanny tomorrow. In the meantime, we need to get a few things for her. I'll help you, Jonah. I'll teach you the basics."

His brown eyes soften as I walk toward him. I'm about to slide pass him in the doorway, but he captures my hands in his. My gaze flies to his, as his warmth arouses the needy spot between my legs.

"Thank you, Quinn. I promise to make it worth your while."

He's not smiling, and gone is his signature 'Body Checker' toughness. In its place I see genuine appreciation, and it messes with me a little, makes it hard for me to stay mad at the guy who spent a lifetime overlooking me as a woman and always challenged me to contests, like he would one of the guys

"You don't have to make it worth my anything," I say, the fight gone out of me. "You're Zander's best friend, and like a brother to me." Okay, not a brother, not even a cousin. More like my brother's hot best friend who just happens to make my ovaries stand up and do the Macarena. Shit. "It's the least I could do," I say.

"Still, I'll make it worth your while somehow or another."

"Okay, fine." I push my short hair behind my ears and glance around. "Let's get this place cleaned up, then we'll run out together and go shopping. I'll help you pick out everything you'll need." I do a mental list. "Wait, did Daisy's mother at least leave a car seat for her."

He shakes his head.

"Dammit."

"How about this," Zander says. "Write me a list and I'll go get the stuff, while you clean this place up."

Isn't that just like my brother, ready to jump in and help. He's a good guy, one full of integrity and character.

"No, we'll go. She's my responsibility, not yours," Jonah's says, and I'm glad to see him step up. He's no doubt worried about me snipping a few of his beloved body parts. "Maybe if you could just pick up a car seat, then bring it back."

"You sure? I don't mind. I mean, I am Daisy's uncle right? Not by blood, but by brotherhood for sure."

"I think I should be the one picking out her things, bro. But thanks. And make sure you get her the best car seat. I don't care what it costs, safety first."

"Okay, I'll grab the seat and be back shortly."

Both Jonah and I nod, agreeing on something, which is a first for us—and a good sign that we'll get done what we need to get done without too many arguments or challenges.

I head into the living room to find a bunch of Jonah's teammates, along with their puck bunnies, making their way downstairs. I pause and give Jonah a look that says they need to go. Now. He winces like I'd just slammed him into the boards as I take sweet little Daisy from Liz, thanking her for helping out.

Jonah grips the back of his neck with one hand and rubs like he's got a massive knot to work out. His T-shirt stretches over tight muscles as he massages, and it takes everything in me not to gawk.

"So, ah, I guess I have some explaining to do," Jonah begins when everyone stares at the baby, all wide eyed and frightened, no doubt praying she's not one of theirs. "Apparently, I have a daughter," he says, and his gaze flashes to mine for a second, like he's waiting for my reaction. I smile at him for finally accepting the fact that sweet Daisy is his. "Found out this morning."

"Congratulations, man," Luke, a teammate known as the Stick Handler says as he steps up to me to take a peek at the sleeping baby. None of the others get too close, probably because they're worried it will rub off on them or something. I resist the urge to roll my eyes.

"So yeah, no parties for a while."

I clear my throat to gain his attention. His eyes flash to mine.

"Or...ever again?" he asks, obviously wondering if that's what the throat clearing meant, which of course, it did.

"Not as long as Daisy is in the house, and she's your responsibility," I say.

I mull that over for a second. Will having a child to care for change him, shift his priorities? I've seen it happen in guys; not hard-core tough guys who've never had to care about anyone but themselves. Well, then again, that's not entirely true. Jonah cares about his best friend. When my brother was down and out with a concussion, Jonah checked on him every day, and I can't forget that when he was at the hospital, he'd visit the children's ward. Giggles would fill the hall...and my heart.

Jonah's buddies and their girls grumble as they gather up their things and file out the front door. Looking like a kicked puppy—like he's never going to have fun again—Jonah shuts it tightly behind him.

"Back in a few," Zander says, rattling his keys, and he and Liz leave through the side door leading to the garage, where he must have parked his car last night.

Jonah turns to me when we're the only two left in the house. "Do you want me to take her from you?" he asks, his voice as shaky as his outstretched hands.

"I think we should lay her down," I say quietly. "Let her sleep."

Jonah scratches his chin. "I don't have a crib yet."

"She doesn't move much at this age. I'd put her in a bed, and secure her with pillows, but I'm guessing all the beds have been slept in."

He gives me a sheepish look. "Ah, yeah."

"Then you get the bedding washed and I'll set her up here on the sofa." I walk across the room and set her down. As I do, I note the way Jonah is studying the way I handle her. She stretches out and I tuck her in, place cushions on the outside of her so she can't roll off. "I'd rather have her close anyway. At least until we get a baby monitor and can hear her cries."

"They neighbors can hear her cries, Quinn," he says, and for some reason that makes me laugh.

"You think that's funny?" he says, his mood lightening slightly. "I thought my head was going to split in two." He pinches the bridge of his nose. "How can something so tiny make so much noise."

"If you're looking for sympathy, forget it. Your headache was your own fault, and you can't drink like that as long as you have Daisy."

"I'm never drinking again," he says and holds his head.

I roll my eyes. Haven't we all been there and said that? "Come on, let's clean. You start upstairs, I'll start here."

We both lose ourselves in our duties for the next hour or so, and from upstairs, I can hear the washing machine going. At least we'll all have clean bedding for tonight. I've never slept over at Jonah's place before. I have my own little condo in the city, close to the daycare where I work. Sometimes, though, when my brother is back home in Massachusetts on hiatus from hockey, I'll stay with him in his mansion just outside of Cambridge. He has a massive property, and most times it's empty. He told me I could stay there anytime I want, even open up a daycare in one of the wings. I've been dreaming of having my own business for years now, but it's his place and I don't want to intrude. Someday he'll want to raise his own family in that house.

Me, well...I'm not interested in a family. I satisfy my maternal instincts at the center every day. Zander, though, he's definitely daddy material. Over the years, he's taken such good care of me, has given me so much, which is why I insist on helping him with Dad's medical bills. It's important for me to make my own way in life, and if Zander doesn't like that, too bad for him. He is, after all the one who made me strong and independent. Now he has to deal with that woman, whether he likes it or not.

I finish gathering up all the garbage, wash and dry the dishes, and take a look in Jonah's fridge. I guess groceries are also on our to-do list today. If I'm staying here, I'm not going on a liquid diet.

The only thing I have left to do is sweep the kitchen floor, but I can't find a broom anywhere. I make my way upstairs, to ask Jonah where he keeps it, and find him in his bedroom, sitting cross-legged on his bed with his laptop open. All this time I've been cleaning, and he's been surfing the net?

Anger sweeps through me. "What do you think you're doing?"

He closes his laptop, like a kid caught with his hand in the cookie jar. Since I'm pretty sure that he was watching porn, or something equally dirty, while I cleaned, I step up to him and open his laptop. My heart jumps into my throat when I see his searches.

Babies. Baby food. Baby clothes. How to take care of a baby.

"Jonah," I say quietly, my heart missing a beat.

He slides his legs from the bed and plants his feet on the floor. "I...just didn't want to look like a total moron, Quinn."

I sit down on the bed next to him. "Look, Jonah. I don't expect you to know anything about babies. You were an only child, and were never around infants."

"I know, but sometimes..." He lets his words fall off.

"Sometimes what?" I push.

"Sometimes, when I do stupid things, you're kind of mean and scary."

I laugh, unable to help myself. "Mean and scary? Are you serious? Jonah, you're known as the Body Checker, one of the toughest guys on and off the ice."

He nods, and I shake my head at him. "You're only five foot tall—"

I stop him. "Five foot two, thank you very much."

"Okay, five foot two, but earlier, you scared the team's two hundred and fifty pound defense man simply by clearing your throat. I mean, I love that you're strong and confident—"

I hold my hand up to stop him. "Wait, you love something about me?" I give a very unladylike snort. "That's a surprise. I thought you *hated* everything about me, especially when I beat you at your own challenges."

"Yeah, well, that's true, but I'm just saying you're a strong woman, with a strong personality."

"Thanks to Zander," I say quietly, not wanting to dwell on the past, or how things could have turned out so differently if it weren't for him.

"When you were younger, I used to think your bark was bigger than your bite," Jonah says, nudging me with his shoulder. I rock against him, and become acutely aware that we're sitting on his bed...his nice, comfy bed.

Don't let your thoughts drift, Quinn.

Suddenly I've visualizing me on the bed, a naked Jonah above me, touching me with those big, calloused hands of his, giving me pleasure unlike anything I've ever felt before.

Shit, I let my thoughts drift.

I clear my throat. "Is that why you called me a Chihuahua?" I ask, trying to keep my voice steady, despite the hot thrum rolling through my body.

His deep brown eyes go wide. "Shit. You knew I called you that?"

I fold my arms and glare at him. "Yeah, I heard it a time or two."

"Hey, it was a compliment." He nudges me again, and I swear to God if he keeps making body contact, I'm going to hand over my panties and beg him to take me.

I give a humorless grunt. "No it wasn't."

"I was wrong though," he says thoughtfully. "I think you can totally handle yourself. You're not a Chihuahua, you're a Ninja Chihuahua."

This time, I burst out laughing. "Seriously, Jonah? Ninja Chihuahua?"

"Hey at least it's better than the names you called *me*. I can't even imagine what you wrote about me in those journals you always had your nose in."

Oh, no, he can't imagine at all.

Thank God.

JONAH

"Are you sure it's secure?" I ask, after reading the instructions and harnessing the baby seat into the back of my car.

"Positive," Quinn says, trying to keep her voice even as she places the baby inside. I'm trying not to drive her crazy with my questions. I know how she can get so annoyed with me, but she's being extra patient this afternoon and for that I'm grateful. I'm not sure how I'll pay her back for all this, but I definitely will. I'd be totally fucked without her.

"This is how you buckle her in," she says, and leans into the car to place Daisy into her seat. For a brief second, my gaze drops to her curvy backside.

Shit. Shit. Shit.

Mind on the task, dude.

I have a baby to take care of, and looking at my best friend's sister's ass—no matter how perfect it is—is not on the agenda. Ever. Not only because she thinks of me as a brother, but staring at her would break the bro code, and that's not going to happen.

The lock snaps into place, and Quinn inches from the car. She tucks a blonde strand of hair behind her ear. "Got it?"

"Got it," I say. I tap my head. "Quick learner."

"Good." She walks to the passenger side and slides in. "I made a list of the things we need most. Crib, stroller, baby monitor, formula, diapers, clothes. We'll start with those things and then move on, purchasing the rest through the week as needed."

I settled myself into the driver's seat, buckle up and back out of the driveway, carefully. "What about one of those baby-on-board signs?"

She laughs, and says, "We can get one of those, too."

I creep down the road, keeping my speed low, never more cautious in my life.

"You can go a little faster," Quinn says. "She's not going to break."

I press the gas pedal, nervous driving with an infant in the vehicle. It takes twice as long for me to reach the mall, but at least the baby wasn't hurt along the way. Jesus, I am so not cut out for children.

I open the back door, and Daisy's eyes are wide open and the brightest blue I've ever seen. Her lip trembles when she sees me and once again she starts to wail.

I jump back, grab a fistful of hair. "She hates me, Quinn," I say, a little unsettled at that.

Quinn removes her from her seat and whispers, "Shh," as she rocks her. Daisy quiets down, and Quinn gives her a pacifier. "She doesn't hate you. She's been with her mother for four months and you're big. She's probably not used to big guys like you. It will just take some time."

"Zander is big too, and she didn't cry when he held her."

Quinn puts her hand on my arm and gives a little squeeze. Goddammit, I should not be thinking about what her soft hand would feel like on other parts of my body. "Give it some time, okay? She'll come around."

I nod, and Quinn continues to hold her as we make our way inside the department store. "She's only four months but she gets heavy after a while."

"Want me to take her?"

"Ah, no. Let's just go pick out a stroller first."

"See, you know she hates me, too. That's why you won't hand her over. You don't want her to cry again."

Quinn laughs. "Stop being a big baby."

I follow Quinn to the baby section, and we pick out furniture and all the other things on her list.

Hours later, Daisy is squirming and crying again, and I'm not even holding her.

"She's hungry," Quinn says, and reaches into the bag she brought with us. Christ, I never would have thought to bring food. The child would starve if I was left alone with her. "Let's find a nursing station."

I have no idea what a nursing station is, or where to find one, but I follow her through the store until we come to a room with numerous other moms and their children. Some of the older kids are playing as mother's nurse their babies, some with bottles and some with their breasts.

Suddenly uncomfortable, I start to back up, but Quinn stop me.

"What do you think you're doing?"

"I don't think I should be in here." I lean down and put my mouth close to her ear, my words meant for her only. "Some of these women have their breasts out."

"You do realize breasts aren't just for a man's pleasure, right?"

"Well...ah..." What the hell can I say? Of course women's breasts are for a man's pleasure? Jesus, I'm such a douche bag. But at least I know it.

She must have come to the same conclusion because she points to a chair, refusing to cut me any sort of slack, and I suppose I should be grateful. "Sit."

"Ninja Chihuahua," I whisper, and Quinn laughs. I do as I'm told, and Quinn places Daisy in my arms. A few of the moms look on curiously.

"Hi," I say to the women, and pray to fuck Daisy doesn't start screeching. She's looking up at me with skeptical big blue eyes, that bottom lip of hers trembling again. I try to bounce her like I'd seen Quinn do, and that's when I notice how goddamn tiny she really is.

"First child?" the woman breastfeeding beside me asks.

"Yeah."

"How old is she?"

"Four months."

"And you're still not comfortable with her?"

I grimace. "Is it that obvious?"

"Don't worry, you won't break her." She smiles at me. "She's tougher than she looks."

That thought makes me sad, because without a mother, it's going to be tough for her. Just like it was tough for Quinn.

Quinn comes back with the bottle and crouches in front of me. She hands the bottle over. "Hold it like this so she doesn't get air bubbles." I do as she says, and Daisy takes big gulping drinks, her tears on hold for the moment.

"She looks like her mom," the woman says. "Big blue eyes."

Quinn smiles and doesn't correct her.

She drinks fast, and when she slows, her eyes slide shut. Quinn takes the bottle from me. "Now you have to burb her."

I put her over my shoulder, the same way Zander had earlier, and I rub and tap her tiny little back. My eyes meet Quinn's and she's watching me carefully, an expression on her face I can't quite figure out. Does she want a baby of her own? Most likely, considering she works in a daycare. But she doesn't go out with many men, has never been serious with anyone. It's not like I keep tabs on her or anything. It's just that she's my best friend's sister and her well-being is important to me.

And yeah, I keep tabs on her.

Daisy lets out the loudest burb in the room and my chest puffs out as the women chuckle. I'm kind of proud that my girl can burb like that.

My girl.

Wow, talk about going from denial to acceptance in record time. But the truth is, I might be a selfish prick, but I had a good upbringing. My mother taught me right from wrong and made sure I accepted responsibility for my actions.

How is she going to feel about little Daisy? My folks are old fashioned and believe in marriage before children. Will they encourage me to marry Shari, to keep a family together? I mean, a baby needs a mom and dad, right? Quinn and Zander know that firsthand. Maybe that's what Quinn was thinking about, that I should go find Shari and do right by her and Daisy.

"We should get her home," Quinn says quietly, her voice a little sad.

I wrap Daisy in her blanket and place her back in the stroller we bought. Since everything we purchased is being delivered, and we were able to do-one stop shopping in the department store, including baby formula, and diapers, we head to the car. Delivery will be later today, which will give me lots of time to get her crib set up before nightfall.

I buckle Daisy in and I cautiously drive to the local grocery store. Quinn seems a little amused by my driving. She averts her gaze and looks out the window. "Are your mom and dad away?" she asks.

"Yeah, they just left, otherwise I wouldn't be taking up all your time with this. I would have gotten Mom to help."

"I don't mind, Jonah. I didn't have much planned for this weekend."

"So, I'm not keeping you from a hot date?" I tease.

I must have touched a sore spot because her head spins my way. "Well, yes, but I can reschedule," she says, and I get the sense she's lying. "Daisy needs me more than I…"

"More than you what?" I ask, wanting to add…*need to get laid*, but I'm not interested in spending the rest of my life with one testicle.

Heat moves into her cheeks, making her look so goddamn sexy, my dick twitches. Goddammit, that's the last thing I need right now.

"More than I need a romantic candlelight dinner out."

"That's your thing? Romantic candlelight dinners?"

"That's none of your business," she says with a lift of her chin.

"You're right, it's not. Want to know *my* thing?"

"I already do. Boobs."

I laugh and catch her grin. "What if I said you were wrong?"

"First, I'd say you were a liar; second, I'd say I don't want to know any more."

"Nothing?"

"No. Nothing. Ever. What kind of weird things you're into is your business, not mine."

We reach the grocery store, and I kill the engine.

"Weird things? What makes you think I'm into weird things?"

She shrugs. "A girl hears things."

"Lies, Quinn. All lies," I say, and she gives me a look that says she doesn't believe me.

We make our way into the store, grab all the supplies

Quinn thinks we need and go back to the car. I drive home, pull into the garage, and Daisy is fast asleep by the time I remove her from her car seat. I'm hoping she doesn't wake up and see me holding her. She's been frightened enough for one day. Once again, anger coils through me. How could Shari just leave her daughter like this?

"Fuck," I say under my breath, then remember I'm not supposed to swear in front of the infant. We get inside, and I set her on the sofa, surrounding her with pillows.

"You *are* a fast learner," Quinn says as she watches me carefully.

"Told you."

"And here I thought you were just a pretty face," she quips.

I step into her, despite knowing better, but I suddenly want to tease her, want to make her blush, because goddammit, there is nothing sexier than Quinn with pink cheeks. I've known it for years. "You think I have a pretty face?"

"No, of course not," she shoots back quickly, her chest rising and falling a bit quicker.

Would you look at that. Little Quinn Reed is flustered. Maybe she's doesn't hate me as much as I think she does. "It's just a saying."

At the risk of losing a testicle, I touch her hair, run it though my fingers. "Too many scars?" I ask.

"No, I'm not shallow," she says, and she reaches out and touches my cheek. "How did you get this one though? Another hockey puck to the face?"

She traces the soft tip of a finger down my cheek, near my ear, and my pulse jumps in my throat. "Fight. High school."

Her eyes widen. "I hate to see what the other guy looks like." She quivers a bit, and pulls her hand back. Under her breath, she says, "I hate violence."

"He sucker punched your brother. It wasn't a fair fight, so he had a broken nose coming to him."

"Oh, I had no idea."

"I protect those I care about, Quinn."

She opens her mouth to say something but from the sofa, Daisy makes a noise, and it pulls me back. *Okay, get your shit together, dude. Hitting on the one girl who can help you out in this messy situation—the one girl you can't put a finger on—is a dick-ass move, on so many levels.*

"Hungry?" I ask.

"Starving," she says quickly, clearly appreciating the change in topic.

"It's going to be a while before Daisy's things and our groceries get delivered. Order in?"

"Sounds like a good idea."

"Italian?" I ask, remembering how much she likes the lasagna from Luigi's.

"Sure." She tugs at her short strands of blonde hair and frowns.

"What?"

"I rushed over here so fast this morning, I didn't have time for a shower. Mind if I use yours."

"Hey, you're here helping me, you can have and use anything you want. I mean anything."

You can even use my body if you're so inclined.

Shit, asshole. Stop thinking like that.

Her big blue eyes go wide, and I suck in my breath. Hoping I didn't say any of that out loud.

"Oh, damn," she says, then covers her mouth and glances at a sleeping Daisy. "Oops."

"What's wrong?"

"We forgot to stop at my place for a change of clothes."

"I can drive you."

"No, I don't want to miss the delivery."

"Did you want to go yourself?" I ask, trying to hide the fact that staying here alone with an infant terrifies me.

She crinkles her nose. "No, I don't really want to leave you alone with her just yet. I mean, I know you can take care of her, but she's not used to you," she says, switching it around to show that it's Daisy she's worried about, but I can't help but think she's worried about me, too.

I almost exhale a breath of relief. "I have some old sweats and a few shirts you can borrow."

She does a sweep of my body, and makes a face. "Nothing of yours is going to fit me."

"I've got sweats that tie, and I've seen you in baggy T-shirts before. Just grab what you need from my closet."

"You don't mind me going through your things?"

"Nope. I'm just like your brother, remember."

She looks away at the reminder, like she doesn't want me to see her expression. "Right. What about a toothbrush?"

"I have spares in the bathroom drawer. Help yourself to anything, Quinn."

She heads toward the stairs. "Am I going to find something...weird...in your closet or drawers?"

"Define weird."

She glances at me over her shoulder, and from her grin, I can tell she's being playful. "Something that one might have to blow up."

I laugh, hard. "You looking for something to blow?" I tease, and her cheeks turn a sexy shade of pink.

"No, I mean...I was just..." She growls, and I grin. Whoever thought I could fluster the Ninja Chihuahua. "Never mind."

She rushes up the stairs, putting an end to my taunting, but hey, she was the one who brought it up. Seriously though, hearing the word *blow* on her lips has my dick standing at attention. Christ, maybe this wasn't such a great idea. Quinn under the same roof as me, sleeping in the next room. Well, that might prove too much.

As Quinn roots around in my closet, I pull my cell phone from my pocket and place an order. Daisy makes sucking sounds, and I drop to the floor beside the sofa. *I'm a dad.* Her tiny fingers are curled, and I tentatively reach out and touch them. She's so little and vulnerable, solely relying on me, and that, I'm not ashamed to admit, scares the living fuck out of me.

Can I do this?

My heart jumps into my throat, and suddenly I'm finding it a little hard to breath.

"You are so tiny," I say quietly. My thumb brushes her soft pink cheek, and she turns toward my hand. "I'm sorry about what your mom did, Daisy. None of this is your fault, and I know I'm not much of a father, but I'm going to try to be the man you need me to be."

Her eyes flicker open, and my heart squeezes as she looks at me, her big blue eyes roaming my face, taking me in, accessing me, like she's seeing me as something different for the first time.

"Hi, Daisy," I say in a soft voice. "I guess I'm your dad." Her lips quivers, and I rush out with, "Yeah, I know, I don't blame you for crying. I would cry too if I were you." I play with her little hand, examine it, and when her tiny fingers fist around one of mine, my heart speeds up and my vision goes a little fuzzy. She makes a cooing sound, and my chest tightens.

The stair creaks, and I lift my head to see Quinn walking back up the steps, her body tight. "Hey," I say.

"I'm sorry." She turns to me. "I didn't mean to intrude or eavesdrop. I just..." She holds up the clothes in her hands. "Wanted to see if it was okay if I wore these."

"Wear whatever you like," I say. "I told you, you can have

and use anything at all. I really appreciate what you're doing for me."

She nods, turns quickly and races up the stairs. After she disappears upstairs again, I grab my phone. There are a ton of messages that I've been ignoring. Damn, news sure travels fast in the hockey circuit. Most of the texts are from the puck bunnies I know, asking if they can come by to help, but I get that's not what they're after. I'm a known player, a guy who plays as hard off the ice as he does on it. These women want one thing from me, and I'm okay with that. I'm not looking to settle down anytime soon, and when I do, I want it to be with someone who sees me as more than the Body Checker. Someone who wants me for me.

I hear a truck pull into the driveway just as the shower turns on upstairs. "Looks like your new furniture is here, little one." I climb to my feet and tuck the blanket tighter around the tired baby as her lids fall shut again, and make my way to the front door.

The driver and his helper unload the first box: Daisy's new crib.

"Hey," I say, and they both greet me with a nod.

The driver nearly drops the box when he reaches the door. "Shit, aren't you—"

"Yeah, Jonah Long," I say. "Better known as the Body Checker."

"Man, you had a great season," his helper says.

"Thanks."

"Where do you want this?" the driver asks.

"Upstairs, second door on the left."

I watch them as they carry the new crib up to Daisy's room, making this fatherhood thing official, and that's when the reality of the situation hits like a stick to the back of the neck.

Jesus, I'm really doing this.

4
QUINN

I turn the shower off and listen to voices outside the bathroom door. I towel-dry my hair, pull on Jonah's sweatpants and soft blue T-shirt and give myself a once over in the mirror. Cripes, I look like stumpy, the eighth dwarf, in his far too big clothes. But beggars can't be choosers, so these things will have to due until I can get to my place tomorrow.

I carefully open one of his drawers, looking for a comb but half expecting to see a box or two of condoms, or some kind of ointment for a rash that has doctors stumped. That thought makes me chuckle.

I grab his comb and run it through my hair and when I'm done, I listen for sound outside the door, and wait until the delivery men are downstairs before I step into the hall. I walk into the bedroom Jonah put the crib in. It's a decent-size room, with a double bed and dresser. It's painted in a soft grey, and I wonder if Jonah might be interested in making it a little more feminine. Not that he'd know how, but I could help him. Then again, maybe it's not in my best interest to spend any more time around him than necessary. The close proximity is messing with my brain and my body.

"Hey," he says, and I nearly jump from my skin.

I turn to him. "Were you trying to scare me?"

He laughs. "No. I was just getting the baby monitor set up."

Still a little bowled over after hearing his private conversation with his daughter—my God, my ovaries were ready to explode—I try to act casual. I plant my hand on my hip and say, "Well, for a big guy, you're kind of stealthy. You should wear a bell or something."

I wait for a response, but instead of coming back with some smart-ass comment, his gaze leaves my freshly scrubbed, makeup-free face, and slowly travels down my body.

I lift my arms and let them flop back to my sides. "I'm probably going to have to sleep naked, otherwise I'll end up strangling myself in these clothes."

His nostrils flare slightly, and that's when I realize what I've said. *Jesus, girl, why are you talking about getting naked in front of Jonah?*

Stupid. Stupid. Stupid.

"Ah, if that's what you want," he says, his voice an octave lower. "Or I could try to find you something smaller." His gaze sweeps over me again, and he scrubs his chin.

Wait, is he picturing me sleeping naked or something? God, I hope not.

Liar.

I shake my head to clear it. Obviously the guy who can get any girl he's ever wanted, who has shown zero interest in me my whole life, is not fantasizing about me naked. That can only be for the best, right?

"It's okay, I'll be fine." Needing to change the subject, I head toward the door. "Which room do you want me in?"

"How about the one across from me? That way if you need me, or I need you, we'll hear each other if we have to call out."

Oh, I can think of all kind of things I need Jonah for. Dirty things. Deliciously sexy things that would likely surprise the Body Checker.

"Sounds reasonable. Are the men gone?" I ask.

He gestures toward the big box leaning against the wall. "Yeah, and I want to get this crib set up right way."

"I can help."

"Our food is here though, so let's eat."

He leaves the room and, as I follow him, I try not to look at his perfect backside, all wrapped up so beautifully in his jeans as we head down the stairs. He glances at me over his shoulder and I'm far too slow to react. When my gaze finally meets his, he has a knowing grin on his face.

Shit.

"I ordered lasagna from Luigi's."

"Oh, my fave."

He gives a nonchalant shrug. "Yeah, I know, that's why I ordered it."

It might mean nothing to him, but my traitorous heart goes a little wobbly at his thoughtfulness. I reach the main level and check on Daisy, who's still sound asleep on the sofa. I grin as I touch her cheek. "She's beautiful, Jonah," I say.

"Thanks," he answers. "Have a seat, I'll bring our plates in."

I take a chair across from Daisy, and Jonah brings me a plate of lasagna and a glass of white wine. "You read my mind," I say as I take the glass from him.

He gives me a lopsided smile that's so damn adorable, I almost forget that I don't like this guy. "I thought you could use a glass, even though you're handling all this better than me."

He disappears into the kitchen, and then comes back with his own plate of lasagna and a glass of water. I'm pleased by that, pleased that he listened to what I had to say this morning about drinking and is trying to do his best.

I bite into the lasagna, and a moan crawls out of my throat. Once again, Jonah's nostrils flare, and he scrubs his chin like he's fighting some internal war.

"Good?" he asks, his teeth clenched.

"The best." I slide my fork into my mouth again—and that's when I become aware of the way Jonah is watching me. I remove the utensil and use it to point at his plate. "Aren't you going to eat?" I ask.

"Yeah." He digs into his lasagna and devours it in record time.

Good Lord, I've eaten around a table with Jonah many times. When did he start shoveling in his food? "Hungry much?"

His fork clatters on his plate as he sets it on the coffee table. "I just want to get started on the crib."

"Let me finish up and I'll help."

"No, it's okay," he says quickly and makes a beeline for the stairs, like he can't get away from me quick enough.

Was it something I said?

I'm not sure, but I'm starving, so I dig back into my food, eating it slowly, because that's way better for digestion. When I'm done, I take our dishes to the kitchen and load them into the dishwasher.

Before heading upstairs, I check on Daisy again, and turn the volume up on the monitor. Papers crinkle as Jonah unfolds the instructions, and I head to the washer and dryer to switch the bedding, tossing Daisy's new crib sheets and blanket into the wash. With a bundle of fresh-smelling sheets in my arms, I walk to my room, directly across from Jonah's master suite, and make up my bed. I smooth my sheets out and sit, noticing I can see straight into his room, an unobstructed view of his bed.

For the briefest of moments, I picture myself between his sheets, his body on top of mine, holding me down and doing the filthiest things to me. A hot blaze rides through my veins, and my hairline grows damp as I envision his mouth on me, those hands touching me in ways that will rock my world. Lord knows my worlds has never been rocked before, but if the rumors about the Body Checker are right—

"Quinn," Jonah calls out, and my thoughts come crashing back to the present.

"Yeah," I say, my voice a little higher than I would have like.

"I need you to hold something for me."

As my thoughts go off in a million different directions, thinking about what I'd like to hold for him, I jump from the bed. "Yeah, sure," I say as I rush into the baby's room.

My feet come to a resounding halt at the doorway.

Holy God. Seeing Jonah all rough and rugged in his hockey gear is one thing, but *this* Jonah, bent down on one knee as he uses an Allen key to screw the bed together, well... that's something else entirely. Something that reminds me I'm a woman, one who hasn't been touched in a very long time.

So what should you do about that, Quinn?

"Can you hold the other end up, so I don't twist the frame?"

I step around him and lift the edge of the crib as he works the tool. "You read the instructions?" I asked.

"I glanced at them, why?"

I shrug. "I don't know. Just wondering."

"It's not rocket science."

"I guess I didn't realize you were so good with your hands.

I mean, I know you can handle a hockey stick, I just didn't think..."

"I'm a *hands-on* kind of guy," he says, and when my gaze flashes to his, catches his devious grin, I swear to God he's talking about sex.

"I put Daisy's sheets in the washer," I say, desperate to change the subject.

"What time do I put her down tonight?"

"Did her mother give any instructions? Do you even know if she's sleeping through the night yet?"

"Nothing. I don't even know how to get ahold of her, either. She just handed Daisy over and left." His teeth clamp together with an audible click, and he grunts. "Pretty shitty thing to do if you ask me," he mumbles through those clenched teeth.

I shake my head, incredulous, and his eyes lock on mine. In that instant, I know we're both thinking the same thing. How can a mother walk out on her child?

How could mine walk out on Zander and me?

I clear my throat. "I guess we'll just have to wing it for the next little bit, until we get her on a schedule. I'm going to make some calls later, to see about a nanny. The sooner we find one, the better."

Jonah finishes tightening the screw and walks toward me. Our hands touch, a soft brush that does the most ridiculous things to the needy spot between my legs.

Since I'm desperate for a man's touch, and he's a man who has the right touch—again, according to the rumors—then maybe I should take advantage of my time here. Scratch an itch while helping him. A tit-for-tat kind of thing.

Jonah is saying something but I'm so lost in my thoughts, I don't hear.

"Quinn," he says, his brows furrowed.

"Yeah."

"Where were you?" he asks, genuine concern in his voice as he waves one hand in front of my face.

"Oh, nothing," I say quickly. "Just thinking about Daisy's mother."

He nods, and he places his hand on my arm, giving it a comforting squeeze, one that doesn't feel brotherly at all. "This must be hard for you, too. Maybe I'm asking too much."

The sadness in his voice curls around my heart. "I'm okay," I say quickly. "I don't mind helping Daisy." I'm not about to discuss my demons with this man. A man I hate. A man I'm thinking about having sex with.

Good Lord, Quinn. Get yourself together already.

Jonah lets the subject drop. If there is one thing he's good at, it's reading a room, and I'm beginning to believe he knows me better than I think he does.

He takes the rail I've been holding and attaches it to the stationary crib side. Once he finishes that, he goes to work on putting the brackets on the base. I stand back for a moment and admire him as he works, take pleasure in the way his muscles ripple and relax again as he steps up to be the man Daisy needs him to be.

"Grab that," he commands in a soft voice and gestures to the rail. I comply, my body quivering slightly as he takes charge. Would he be as demanding in the bedroom?

A noise I have no control over crawls out of my throat.

"You okay?"

"Ah, yeah, just twisted my finger," I fib.

"Let me see." As he stands over me, taking my hand to examine it, I become acutely aware of his size, his hardness, our close proximity. His eyes narrow. "Which finger?"

I hold out my index...and he brings it to his mouth, dropping a soft kiss onto the tip.

My entire body comes alive, and I jerk my hand back. "What...what are you doing?"

His head rears back. "Jesus, sorry. I don't know why I did that." He grips the back of his neck, a familiar habit when he's uncomfortable. "That's what my mom used to do when I was a kid, and maybe having Daisy here is just messing with me. I shouldn't have touched you."

"It's okay, Jonah. We've touched a million times."

"Not like that," he says, as we both stand there, staring at each other, tension taking up space between us.

I finally break the moment and say, "We better get this done before Daisy wakes up."

"Right," he says, stepping back, the spell between us broken.

I help him lift the base and attach it to the crib ends. As he tightens all the screws, I stand back and look at the pretty white sleigh crib.

"It's perfect," I say, and don't miss the longing in my voice. God, what is going on with me today? I resigned myself to the fact that I wasn't going to have a family of my own a long-ass time ago. Yet in the span of one day, Daisy has tugged at all my maternal instincts.

Jonah stands and crosses his arms. He nudges me. "Good job."

I laugh. "I didn't do much."

Just then, Daisy's cries come through the monitor.

"Is she hungry again?" he asks, his body going tense.

"Or she needs a diaper change."

He looks at me, and I've never seen such horror on a man's face before. I do my best not to laugh at him.

"I'm not doing that," he says adamantly.

"Oh, yeah you are," I say, and put my arm through his. I give him a tug but he doesn't budge. Jesus, he's strong.

"Quinn..." There is pleading in his voice.

"Come on, you have to learn. I'm not always going to be here to help you out, you know."

"How long will you be here?" he asks, and for the briefest of seconds, his look isn't one of fear, it's longing.

Longing?

Okay, I'm definitely losing my mind. Daisy being here isn't just affecting him, it's messing with me, too. No way would Jonah look at me with longing, right? This is my brother's best friend. The NHL's Body Checker. A different girl in his bed every night.

"Until we get a nanny. Someone we're both comfortable with," I say, then exit the room. I hurry down the stairs, and Jonah is on my heels.

Daisy is wailing by the time we reach her, and Jonah stands over her, panic on his face once again. My heart softens, and while I'd like to just go ahead and take care of Daisy, Jonah has to learn.

"Hey there, little one," I say, having heard Jonah call her that earlier. "Do you need a diaper change?" I remove the blankets and tuck one underneath her. The changing table is still in a box so we'll have to make due.

"Grab me the baby wipes and a diaper from the bag," I say, and Jonah obliges. He plunks himself down on the coffee table to watch, and I show him how it's done. "It's easy," I say. "You just unpeel the tape here, lift her legs to pull it out, the roll it up and re-tape." I pull a couple wipes from the bag, clean her up, and slide a new diaper under her. "The tape goes around the back," I explain. I finish changing her and take her into my arms.

Jonah has a sweat going on when I stand and head to the kitchen for her bottle.

"Okay, that doesn't seem so hard."

I hand the baby over to him and wash my hands before I get her bottle from the fridge, and when I turn back, catching the way he's looking at his daughter, my heart melts. They might not have had any bonding time before now, but I give it a few days before the two fall totally in love.

A yawn pulls at me as we walk into the living room, and I hand Jonah the bottle. He sits, and feeds her the way I taught him. I flick on the TV, find some old rerun and half watch it. The washer beeps, and I rush upstairs and switch the sheets.

When I come back down again, I find Joan with his head back, his eyes closed, and Daisy in his arms. I'm pretty sure both are sound asleep. I smile at that and lower the volume on the TV. But sleep pulls at me too. I flick through the stations, wasting time until the bedding is done. When the dryer finally finishes, I make Daisy's bed and head back downstairs.

"Jonah," I say quietly, and his eyes open. Dark brown eyes lock with mine, and for a moment he looks confused. "We need to put Daisy to bed."

He nods and cradles the baby in his arms. "Right."

"Here, let me take her." I reach for the bundle as he stands. He stretches out.

"What time is it anyway?"

"It's just a little after eight. But I think we can both use a good night's sleep."

We head upstairs, and I give Daisy a kiss on the cheek before I place her in her crib. She makes a little gurgling sound, and Jonah steps up to me and covers her. His hands so big next to his daughter's, but so soft and gentle as he touches her. My poor ovaries are going to explode before I can get a nanny in here.

We leave her door cracked so we can hear her and I head to my room, expecting Jonah to go to his.

"I think I'm going to put a few more things together."

"Okay, don't be up too late. I suspect that little girl is an early riser."

I make a quick trip to the bathroom, then go to bed, but don't close my door all the way, just in case Daisy or Jonah need me through the night.

Even though I'm tired, sleep doesn't come, partly because of the craziness of the day, and partly because Jonah is still up assembling the small dresser and changing table that matches Daisy's new bed.

A long while later, Jonah's footsteps sound in the hall. They pause outside my door, and I suck in a quick breath. With my door cracked, he can see me. Should I let him know I'm awake?

Before I can make that decision, he walks into his bedroom, and I peek over the covers, see him move around in his room. He peels off his shirt, and I cover my mouth to stop the moan rising in my throat. My God, the man has one gorgeous body.

He reaches for the button on his jeans, and I pinch my eyes shut. It's wrong to look, right?

I inch one eye open just as he peels his pants from his legs and tosses them over a chair.

Look away, Quinn. Look away.

I don't look away.

No, instead, I watch him strip and disappear into his master suite bathroom for a shower. I resist the urge to sneak in, watch him soap his gorgeous body. Jesus, I'm turning into a regular old voyeur. But when it comes right down to it, there is no denying I want to feel that man's touch, and in turn put my hands on his rock-hard body.

But that wouldn't be wise. No, not wise at all.

JONAH

I toss in my bed, unable to shut down my mind. It's not much wonder. When I woke up this morning, my only plans for the day were to nurse a damn hangover. Never in a million year would I have guessed that Shari would drop a baby into my arms, or that Quinn would be sleeping in the room across from me.

I lift my head slightly and glance out into the hallway. Her door is cracked but her room is dark, so I can't tell if she's awake or not. Unlike me, she's probably fast asleep, not fantasizing about what it would be like to be in bed together, doing all the things I've dreamt about doing to her since she grew curves at sixteen. Christ, she's by far the sexiest girl I've ever set eyes on. But she's in the hands-off zone, and I damn well plan to keep it that way, no matter how much my cock is begging me to go in there and put my mouth on her sexy body.

It's the wee hours of the morning and sleep finally pulls at me. I allow my lids to drift shut, my mind to settle, when a loud cry rips through my slumber, jolting me awake.

I jackknife up in the bed, try to orient myself, figure out

where the crying is coming from. That's when I remember Daisy is in the next room. I tug on a pair of boxer shorts and hurry to my daughter's room.

My daughter.

Christ, I'm not sure I'll ever get used to that. Her cries grow louder, almost frantic, and I pick her up, settle her against my bare chest. The child is so confused and frightened, it tugs at the protector in me, and once again I'm angry that Shari just left her like this.

"It's okay, little one," I whisper quietly, not wanting to wake Quinn, but wanting to wake her just the same because I am so out of my element here. "Are you hungry, need a diaper change?"

"She probably needs both," a soft voice says from behind me.

I turn to see Quinn leaning against the doorjamb. "Hey, sorry we woke you."

"It's okay." Light from the hall filters in and Quinn narrows her eyes as she looks at me. "Did you get any sleep?"

"Not much."

She crosses the room and holds her arms out. "Why don't you give her to me and go back to bed. I'll take care of her tonight."

"No, you go back to bed, I got this." Okay, that's not entirely true. I don't *got this*, and I don't want Quinn to go back to bed. I really need her.

She shakes her head, not believing me for a second. Thank God. "You want to change her, or get the bottle?"

I quickly hand her over, and Quinn chuckles. "That's what I thought."

I head for the door as she walks to the changing table, the room a bit tight with the double bed still in it. I'm going to have to get rid of it and make the space more suitable.

"The table looks nice," she says, and then she stifles a yawn.

"Thanks." I hurry down the stairs and prepare Daisy's bottle, checking the temperature on my arm like I'm a pro. I'm not. I'm so not equipped to take care of a child, and scared fucking shitless because I have no choice now.

Daisy is still bawling, and Quinn is humming to her as she finishes changing the diaper and dressing her. I wait at the doorway for a second, the sight totally catching me off guard. I never thought about having kids before, or a wife. I guess it was always just off in the distance, something to think about later, but the vision is fucking me over a little, tugging at something deep inside—scaring me even more.

"Hey," I say quietly as I step up to Quinn. Her body tightens as I reach around her, my chest against her back, and I put the bottle into Daisy's mouth and hold it there. Daisy gulps fast.

"She eats like you do," Quinn says quietly, as she rubs her hands over the child's legs.

I laugh. "All she does is eat...and cry."

"It will get better," she assures me. "Soon, she'll start sleeping through the night, and just wait until she develops a personality."

Quinn steps away from me, and I don't want to think too hard on how much I miss her closeness. I pick Daisy up and sit on the edge of the bed to feed her. Quinn lowers herself down next to me.

"I think she's getting used to you already."

I nod, not quite sure I believe that. She's just happy to be getting her bottle. "Quinn?"

"Yeah."

"I...I really appreciate you being here. For Daisy's sake."

A moment of silence and then, "My pleasure."

Daisy drinks and drinks and drinks, and when half the

bottle is gone, I put her over my shoulder and tap her back to burp her.

She burps all right—only problem is, she loses half her milk down my back.

"Jesus," I whisper, as my entire body tightens. "She just threw up on my back." My hand stills midair. "Wait, am I burping her too hard?" I try to keep the worry from my voice. "Am I doing something wrong?"

"No." Quinn grabs some baby wipes from the plastic container and runs them over my back. "Sometimes babies just have wet burbs. It's normal."

"You sure?"

"Yes, I'm sure. Give her the rest of her milk, and I'll get a soapy cloth to clean you."

I readjust her in my arms and put the bottle in her mouth, but she doesn't want any more. She turns her head, pushes it away, and her fists are flying.

"Quinn, hurry," I say, and she comes rushing back in. "What's wrong with her?"

"I don't know." She runs the wet cloth over my back, and her hands graze my skin.

"Thanks." I stand and gently bounce the baby in my arms.

"I wonder if she's teething, or maybe she's colicky," Quinn says.

"Maybe she misses her mom," I say.

"Yeah, maybe."

I walk her, and she eventually settles in my arms.

"Let's put her back in her crib," Quinn says, and the second I lay her down, she starts crying again. I pick her up quickly and hold her to my bare chest. It seems to settle her.

"Do you have a rocking chair?" Quinn asked.

"No, but I'll get one tomorrow if you think I need one."

"I think little Daisy is confused and needs the contact right now. But you can't stay up and hold her all night." She peels the comforter from the bed. "Why don't you try to lay down with her here, keep her close to your body."

I do as she says, and Daisy coos and closes her eyes.

"I think she just needed her daddy," Quinn says.

"I can't sleep like this. What if I roll over and squish her?"

"How about this. I'll sit up for a while and watch. When Daisy falls into a deep sleep, I'll put her in her crib and leave you where you are."

"I don't want to keep you up." Well, that's not entirely true. I *do* want to keep her up, in so many other ways.

She crosses the room, sits on the bed and leans her back against the headboard. "I'm sure it won't be long," she says—and that's when I finally notice she's in nothing but my long T-shirt. Before I can help myself, my eyes travel the length of her, note her bare legs, the way the shirt rides up on her thighs as she stretches her hands over her head.

Motherfucker.

I close my eyes, settle myself on the pillow, and keep one hand on Daisy, just to let her know she's not alone. She gurgles and falls asleep. I close my eyes, not convinced I'm going to sleep, not with Quinn on the other side of the bed...

But when I open them again, Quinn is just putting the baby into her crib.

"How long have I been asleep?" I ask quietly, and rub the blur from my eyes.

"About half an hour. I think this little one is out for the night. Why don't you go back to your own bed, now that you're awake. You'll probably sleep better."

I stand, and Quinn's gaze drops, taking in my boxer shorts.

"It was all I could find when Daisy started crying," I say, feeling the need to explain. The fact that they're tenting as I gaze at the beautiful woman dressed in my shirt, well...that doesn't quite need any explanation.

She turns from me, and I follow her out the door. Quinn lowers the dimmer switch in the hall, and we make our way to our rooms. She pauses for a second outside her door, looks at me like she wants to say something, then darts inside.

"G'night."

I make my way to my own room and flop down on my bed. I check my phone, read the messages from Zander, and shoot him one back telling him we're good. I set the phone on my nightstand and hope sleep will come.

I toss and turn, unable to shut down my thoughts. All I can think about is taking my cock into my hands as I visualize Quinn in bed with me, my mouth between her legs, eating at her, sating far too many years of need. My mind goes on an erotic journey, and I spend the next twenty minutes pictures all the dirty things I want to do to my best friend's kid sister—the one girl who is off limits to me.

Sexually frustrated, I climb from my bed and walk quietly downstairs, needing to wet my parched throat.

I grab a glass of water and open the fridge. When I see the leftover lasagna, I pull it out. I drop it onto the island and grab a fork.

Just then, I hear footstep, and glance up to see Quinn tiptoeing into the kitchen. My dick thickens as soon as I see her, and I revel in the way my T-shirts brushes over her nipples as she walks.

"Everything okay?" she asks.

"Yeah, I was just thirsty."

"And hungry," she points out with a grin.

"Always hungry, just like Daisy," I say.

Her chuckle is soft, low. "Okay, good. I checked on Daisy and she's still sleeping." She makes a move to go, but for some reason, I don't want her to leave.

"Want a bite." I scoop up a piece of lasagna and hold it out.

"I normally don't have carbs this late," she says, and crinkles her nose, but the hunger in her eyes as she looks at my forks tells another story. She wants a bite.

"We're not operating under normal circumstances here, Quinn."

She laughs, a deep, throaty sound that wraps around my dick and tugs. "I suppose one bite wouldn't hurt."

She slides onto the chair across from me, and I hold the fork out. She hesitates for a second then leans forward, and lets me feed it to her. Her lips part, and her eyes slip shut as I slide the lasagna in and, so help me, it's all I can do not to order her to her knees and feed her something else, something that's swelling between my legs and demanding attention.

Fuck me.

"Mmm," she moans.

Before I can help myself, I say, "Can you stop making that noise?"

Her lids flick open. "What noise?"

"The moaning. You do it a lot."

"I always make that noise when I'm enjoying something."

"Yeah, well, it's kind of fucking turning me on," I confess without thinking.

Shit, what are you doing dude?

Her eyes go wide and she sinks deeper into her seat. "Oh, I...didn't realize."

We stare at one another for a moment, my appetite for the lasagna long gone.

"You were right," I say, my voice a little deeper than it was moments ago.

She lifts her chin, but she still seems a bit disconcerted from my confession. "Of course I was."

I laugh. "Don't you want to know what I'm talking about?"

She looks a bit hesitant, then she takes the fork from me and digs into the lasagna. "Okay, enlighten me."

What I'm about to say isn't smart, and I'm probably going to lose my left nut—and my best friend—but with my blood rushing south, I'm not sure I can stop myself. "You were right about boobs being my thing."

My gaze drops, and hers follows, to take in the twin peaks on her shirt. Since the house is warm—I jacked the heat to inferno for Daisy's sake—there can be only one thing making her nipples that hard.

She fucking wants me as much as I want her.

Her hand quivers slightly as she sets the fork back into the lasagna tray. "Yeah, most guys are boob men," she says, her voice hitching a little.

I'm pretty sure she has no idea where this is going, but I sure as fuck do...and if I knew what was good for me, I'd end this right now. *Just go back to bed and rub one out already.*

"Since we're being honest, what part of a guy do you like best?" I ask, in a calm manner that belies the storm going on inside of me.

So much for doing what's good for me.

Her gaze drops quickly, zeroes in on my abs.

"Ah, an abs girl."

Her gaze flickers back to me, and her cheeks are pink, like she's given away too much. "No. I mean...yes."

"Which is it, Quinn? Are you an abs girl or not?"

"I like abs but that's not it. I actually don't know what you call it."

"Show me." I step around the counter until I'm beside her. I grip her chair and spin her until she's facing me.

She lifts her hand, tentative at first, like she might be afraid to touch me, but then her hand goes to my oblique muscles, and she runs the soft pad of her index finger along the length of one.

"Right here," she says.

"Oblique muscles," I tell her.

She chuckles, but it's full of unease and desire.

"Something funny?" I ask.

"No. Well...it's just they almost look like an arrow, guiding the eyes...or hands," she says, as her fingers go lower, linger over the band of my boxers. "Down there."

"Down there?" I tease. "Down where, Quinn?"

She pulls her hand back like I'd just slapped it. "You know where."

I angle my head and grin at her. "You can't say it."

She lifts her chin in a defiant manner, and I have to say, it's a look that turns me on. Always has. Weird fuck that I am. "I can say it. I've said it tons of times."

She's lying, and we both know it.

"Are you saying you like to talk dirty?"

She swallows, and the sound curls around us. "Yes."

"Then do it," I challenge.

"Fine, they look like arrows guiding the eyes or the hands to your cock," she says, accepting my challenge. I'm not surprised. Quinn never was one to run away from a good dare, which is why she broke her arm at sixteen when I bet I could climb higher in a tree than her. I still feel pretty shitty about that. "Happy now?" she asks.

"Happy? I'm not sure that's the word I'd use to explain how I'm feeling right now."

I move closer, touch her hair, and brush the backs of my knuckles over her cheek as I run the soft, silky strands through my finger.

"Then what *are* you feeling?" she asks, her voice as shaky as her body.

Since she opened that door, I decide to step through and go for broke. "Aroused."

6

QUINN

Aroused.

Sweet Mother of God.

Unable to help myself, I let my gaze slide downward—and nearly fall off my chair when I see his erection tenting his shorts, struggling to get free.

Jonah is aroused...because of me.

So what the hell am I going to do about that?

My mouth waters, and my hands itch to touch him as he invades my personal space, the enticing scent of his skin doing the craziest things to my body. I breathe in his fresh, soapy scent and a soft little moan catches in my throat.

"You're making that noise again," he whispers.

"Sorry."

Not sorry.

He quirks a questioning brow, and I know him well enough to knows he's going to challenge me, like he always used to do when we were kids. "Does it mean you're enjoying something?"

"I...uh..."

Exactly how do I respond to that? I'm never one to back

down from a challenge, and saying yes might get me into his bed. But what if he's just messing with me, teasing me like he used to do when we were kids?

He puts his hands on my knees and leans in, his mouth right there. If I wanted to kiss him, all I'd have to do is move an inch.

I want to kiss him.

"Well, does it?" he presses.

Okay, girl, if there was ever a time you needed to meet a challenge, take a chance, now is it.

I take a fueling breath, and brush my tongue over my bottom lip.

"Yes," I say. "It does mean I'm enjoying something."

A small smile plays on his mouth—and in an instant, I understand he's not messing with me. Jonah Long wants me.

Jonah Long wants me.

"What are you enjoying, Quinn?"

With that knowledge, I reach out, never so bold in my life, and place my hand over his engorged cock, loving the long length of him. My sex quivers, desperate to be pleasured by this man, to experience his brand of lovemaking. If the rumors are true, I'm in for one hell of a night.

"I'm enjoying this," I say, and give him a little massage.

A deep growl rips from his lungs.

"Does that sound mean *you're* enjoying something, too?"

"Fucking right it does." He closes his hand over mine, applies more pressure to his cock, and moves his hips.

I moan again, and his other hand goes to my breast. He cups it, lightly runs his thumb over my turgid nipple. Damn, that feels good. I arch into him, letting him know in no uncertain terms that I want this.

"You look hot in my clothes, Quinn."

"Don't you think they're a bit big?" I ask, my voice coming out a breathless whisper as his thumb strokes me, the sensations running through my body and settling deep between my legs.

Before I realize what he's doing, he has his hands around my waist and is lifting me until I'm sitting on the island, the marble counter cool against my bare legs.

He forcefully pushes my legs open and slides in between them. Damn, who knew I'd like this take-charge alpha side of him so much? His hand slides up my back, goes to my hair, and he tugs. My mouth opens, and his lips come down over mine.

A gasp catches in my throat as he devours me, his mouth moving over mine, hard, hungry, demanding. Our tongues tangle, and his slashes against the sides of my mouth, tasting me deeply. The man kisses like a God, and I'm breathless, panting when he breaks it.

He cups my breasts again. "I want my mouth here," he says.

Needy girl that I am, I grip the hem of the shirt and peel it over my head. He chuckles at my eagerness. But then he steps back, his gaze raking over me like a hot caress. Dressed in nothing but my panties, I squirm on the countertop, my entire body beckoning his. His eye meet mine, dark, needy, ravenous, and my lungs compress. My God, he's going to eat me alive.

I briefly close my eyes, suddenly not sure if I'm ready for a guy like him.

"I take it you need that too?" he asks, and when my lids flicker open, and I see the raw hunger on his face, a new kind of need rips through me.

My brain shuts down, and with desire ruling my actions, I reach for him. "Yes, Jonah. Please..." My God, I've never begged for a man's touch in my life. Then again, I've not been with many men...and never any like the Body Checker.

"I like a girl who knows what she wants."

"Do you?" I ask, and grip his hair to guide his mouth to my breasts, showing him exactly what I want. His laugh vibrates through me, and I quiver when his hot mouth closes over my aching nipple. He sucks, and my pale nub swells even more beneath his deft ministrations.

"Jonah," I say as he nibbles on my nipple then clenches down slightly until pleasure mingles with pain. A gasp tears from my lungs at the duel assault. Honest to God, I've never felt anything quite like it. My sex clenches, and my entire body ignites as his hands roam my nakedness, a hurried exploration of my body, like he can't get enough of me.

He treats my other breast to the same pleasure, and his mouth is wet when he breaks from my body and presses his forehead to mine, his breath coming faster, spilling over my face.

"You should probably know, boobs aren't my only thing," he says, pressing hot, open-mouthed kisses to my forehead, nose, eyes and cheeks.

"No?" I ask, playing along, even though I'm not so sure it's wise with a guy like Jonah, but I'm too far gone, too damn needy to turn back now.

"No, I'm into many other things."

"Such as?" I ask, my entire body vibrating, anxious to find out.

"Oh, you suddenly want to know now, do you?"

"Yes," I say, unable to keep the desperation from my voice.

"Okay, then." He slides his hand up my thigh and grips my lace panties. "Why don't you lift, and I'll show you."

I brace my hands on the counter and lift my ass, allowing him to lower my panties to my thighs. He wiggles them down, his calluses scraping my bare flesh and sending shivers skittering through me as he removes the scrap of material and proceeds to twirl them around his finger.

"Black lace," he murmurs. "Sexy, but I was hoping you were naked underneath my shirt."

He reaches between my legs, strokes me softly, and a growl catches in his throat. "You've been thinking about me touching you like this?" he asks.

"Jonah," I say, sexual frustration lacing my voice as he teases me, circling my clit but never quite touching.

"You might as well admit it, Quinn. Just look at your panties...look how wet they are." He runs his finger along my length, presses into my opening, and I moan. "Don't lie to me. I *feel* how wet you are."

As I stare at him, I'm fully aware that there is no sense in denying it. I want his touch, and my wetness is a dead giveaway. "I've been thinking about you touching me," I admit. I take in his dark eyes, and just hope he doesn't ask how long I've been fantasying about us together like this. He doesn't need to know that it goes back many years. Since he always overlooked me, I pretended to hate him. That was easier than rejection.

He's not rejecting you now, Quinn.

No, he's not. He's looking at me with hunger, worship even. I'm certain this is a one-night thing. Come tomorrow, when we're not overcome with lust, we'll both come to our senses and realize this wasn't smart. But tonight—oh, tonight, I plan on taking full advantage of our bad choices.

"The second I saw you in these boxers, I became wet," I admit, deciding to hold nothing back.

He grins. "See, that wasn't so hard, was it? And since you're being honest, I will be too." He runs a finger over my sex, and finally, *finally*, strokes my swollen clit, and my hips come off the counter. He sucks in a breath, a tortured look on his face, like it's taking every ounce of strength he has to keep it together. "Earlier tonight, I almost took my cock in my hands and jacked off as I thought about burying my mouth between your legs and eating you."

"That's..." I begin, my body visually quaking. "That's what you're into?" I ask, and don't miss the anticipation in my voice.

"Oh, yeah. That's exactly what I'm into."

He pulls my hips forward and puts my legs over his shoulders. A little whimper catches in my throat as he leans into me and run his tongue along my slit. I grip his hair and shamelessly rub against him.

"Jonah," I cry out, as he expertly pleasures me with his mouth, eats at me like he'd been living on rations. My eyes slide shut, and the room closes in on me, nothing mattering but this man and the way he's devouring me. He moans, a telltale sign that he loves what he's doing as much as I love him doing it. He runs the long length of his tongue over me, then pushes it inside my sex. Mumbled curses reach my ear, and for a second I can't believe Jonah is between my legs, giving me pleasuring unlike any other man ever has.

"So good!" I cry out, and wiggle. He grips my hips, holds me still, keeping me at his mercy as he feasts on me. His tongues swirls around my clit, laps at it, and then, oh God, and then he slides one finger into me—and with that first sweet touch to my G-spot, a dam burst inside my body, and a hot flood of need, many long years in the making, spills out of me.

I gasp for breath, claw at the man licking me, each clench more intense than the first, overwhelming me in ways that are a bit frightening.

"Jonah," I say when I can finally find my voice again, my nails dragging skin as I run my hands over his back. He stays between my legs a moment longer, touching me softly, licking me gently.

I grip his shoulders, needing my mouth on him. He stands

and slides his hands around my body, pulling me to him... claiming me.

"I want you on my bed, legs open." He pulls me onto his hips, and I wrap my legs and arms around him as he carries me up the stairs like I weigh nothing. We step into his room, and he closes the door quietly behind us.

He carries me to his bed, and I slide down his body. My feet hit the floor, but I don't stop there. I continue down and kneel in front of him, glance at his poor tortured cock trapped in his boxers.

"Quinn," he growls. "Jesus fuck, Quinn. What are you doing?"

I stroke him through his boxers, and he's as hard as granite. "I thought I'd show you some other things that *I'm* into," I say. While it's not entirely true, I never really enjoyed this with the few men I've been with, for some odd reason, I can't wait to put Jonah's cock in my mouth.

"You on your knees like this...I might fucking explode down your throat." I quake at that. "But I won't. Not this time."

Disappointment settles in my stomach. "No?"

He grips my hair and tugs until my mouth is open, and I'm starting to understand how much he likes me like this. "Because there are so many other things I want to do to you tonight, and when I come, I want to be inside your sweet pussy."

I gulp, wanting that too.

His hips sway, and I grab the elastic on his boxers and tug them down. His cock jerks forward, slaps my face, leaves a streak of pre-cum on my lips. I brush my tongue over my bottom lip to taste him, and the grip in my hair tightens. Jonah is losing it. That thought fills me with power. *I'm* doing this to him. Me, Quinn Reed, the girl he always overlooked and challenged when we were young. Damn, I like that. Maybe a bit too much.

Wanting to rattle him just a bit more, I say, "Have you been thinking about me on my knees like this, your cock so deep in my mouth it's practically down my throat?"

His entire body trembles, and I lean forward to lap at his crown, drink in the rest of his pre-cum.

"Quinn, Jesus," he grumbles, a warning lingering behind his words.

Deciding to put him out of his misery—I mean, after all, he'd just given me the best orgasm of my life—I widen my mouth even more and offer it up to him.

He grips his cock, strokes it a few times, then slowly slides into my mouth, feeding me an inch at a time until I choke a little. He pulls out, but I grip his ass and hold him there, wanting to take as much as I can.

He rocks with me, and I work my mouth over him, enjoying the tangy taste of his skin. I moan around his cock, loving what I'm doing, and he thickens even more. I remove one hand from his ass and cup his balls, gently massage them in my palm. His breathing is harsh now, labored, and it's clear he's fighting to do one of two things—pull from my mouth when it obviously feels so good, or come down my throat.

"That's fucking good," he murmurs, and I suck on his crown, and work my hand over his long length. A second later, I'm on my feet...and when my gaze meets dark, intense eyes, a man so close to losing it, I lower myself onto the bed, and open my legs for him.

"Are you going to fuck me now?" I ask.

"Yeah," he says, and grips his cock. He works his hand over it for a moment, his eyes never leaving my sex. "You ready for me to fuck you, Quinn?"

He looks so carnal and possessive, I know I'm in over my

head, and for a brief second I think about running away. What is this man going to do to me?

I'm not sure, but I guess I'm about to find out.

"Yes," I murmur, and move back on the bed, giving him room to climb on with me. My body is quivering, and my pussy is clenching just from watching him stroke his long, thick length.

"You want my cock in you, making you feel so fucking good?"

"I do."

"Show me where you want it?" His gaze leaves mine, travels to the needy juncture between my legs. I touch my breasts, rub my nipples for a second, then move my hands to my sex. I open my damp lips, completely exposing my most private parts to him and shocking myself at how bold I am with this man.

"Right here," I say as he opens his nightstand drawer and pulls out a condom. "I want your cock inside my pussy."

His nostrils flare, every muscle in his body taut as he climbs on the bed, grabs my legs and widens them even more. He lightly strokes me, pushes a finger inside, and fucks me like that a few times.

I ride his finger, but it's not enough. I want his cock.

"This sweet cunt," he begins, "I want it so much, I just might ruin you."

Breath leaves my lungs in a whoosh, his dirty words stroking me deeply. "Yes," I whisper for lack of anything else.

"You need to be taken by me, Quinn?"

Without waiting for a response, he tears into the condom and quickly sheathes himself, then he falls over me, his mouth finding mine. I taste myself on his lips as his mouth eats at mine. His crown probes my opening, and I move my hips, trying to force him inside. His pushes my hands over my head, and holds them there with one of his as the other goes to my breast.

He brushes my nipple with his thumb as he powers into me, one quick thrust that pulls a cry of pleasure from my lungs.

He seats himself high, gives me a moment to adjust then moves his hips, driving in and out of me, a fast, maddening pace that shuts down my ability to think with any sort of clarity.

"Yes," is all I can manage to say, and when he lets my hands go and grips my shoulders for better leverage, I put my hands on his damp back, take pleasure in his hard muscles as he fucks me...like a god.

"You're so fucking tight," he growls into my ear before he buries his face into the hollow of my throat, his tongue gliding over my skin.

Each thrust takes me higher and higher, and my hips come off the bed to grind against him, a shameless exhibit of need. Little electrical currents move through my body, center on my sex, and when his pubic bone connects with my clit, my muscles clench around his cock, an explosion of passion.

"Motherfucker," he swears, as my hot release drips down my thighs and coats his balls. He pumps once, twice, then throws his head back and stills inside me. I hold him to me, and concentrate on each vibrating pulse.

When his body finally stops spasming, he collapses on top of me, and I wrap my legs around him, holding him to me, never wanting this night to end.

He lifts his head, cups my face and pushes my hair from my forehead. His eyes meet mine. "You good?" he asks, his voice so full of tender concern, I have to take a quick second to remind myself this is just sex. Two people scratching an itch.

"I'm good," I say. "You?"

"Yeah." He rolls off me and drags me with him, until I'm snuggled against his chest. After a long moment, he breaks the quiet. "Quinn?"

My heart races. Is this where he brushes me off, tells me to go back to my own room? The Body Checker's moves are well known, and the truth is, I knew what I was getting into when I seduced him. Or rather, he seduced me. I'm not quite sure how that all went down. But the reality is, I know he has a revolving door, and women don't sleep over. When I arrived this morning—was it only this morning?—whoever he was with the night before was long gone.

"Yeah?" I say, and make a move to go.

He drags me back, a possessive tug, and I glance up at him, confused.

He doesn't make eye contact; instead he puts his arm over his eyes and mumbles, "Next time you're in my clothes, I don't want you wearing panties. When I lift your shirt, I want to find you bare and ready to be fucked, okay?"

Oh. My. God.

JONAH

I look at the woman sleeping beside me and can't believe that we fucked last night. And oh, how we fucked. My cock thickens from the memories. It was seriously the hottest sex of my life, and her talking all dirty like that nearly blew my mind and my load.

But seriously, what the hell was I thinking?

I wasn't. That much is obvious. Did I really tell her that the next time she's in my clothes, I want her naked underneath? Talk about some big fucking balls. Balls her brother is likely going to cut off and feed to me if he ever finds out. Then again, he's the one who called her to help me, so part of the responsibility is his.

How is that for logical reasoning at its worst?

I glance at the clock. It's eight in the morning. My thoughts turn to my daughter. *My daughter.* Is she still asleep? She must be, otherwise she's be crying her eyes out. Not that I can blame her. She had a pretty traumatic day yesterday. I have a billion concerns, things I need to think of, plans I need to make, but it's so goddamn overwhelming, I try to block it out for now, just take this fatherhood thing one day, one hour, at a time.

I ease from the bed, pull on a pair of sweatpants, and tiptoe quietly from the room. I listen outside Daisy's door and when I hear cooing noises, I inch it open, praying to God the sight of me doesn't send her into hysterics again. I walk to her crib, and she's staring at the ceiling, her feet and hands moving. Her eyes move to mine, and when her chin quivers, I act quickly, wanting to soothe her worries.

"Hey, little one," I say quietly, and she watches me with those big blue eyes, so unsure of me. I don't blame her. I'm unsure of me, too. "Are you hungry?" I ask, as I cradle her against my chest. Her little head bobs against my body, then she glances up at me, like she's trying to figure out if she likes me or not.

Her diaper feels soggy beneath my hand, so before I feed her, I need to change her. I place her on the changing table, and talk quietly to her. "If you're wondering who I am and what I do, well, I'm your daddy, apparently, and sorry that was just sprung on you. It was sprung on me, too. Anyway, I'm a hockey player. When you get bigger, I can teach you how to play, too." I frown. "That is if you want to. Maybe you want to be a dancer or something." I unsnap the bottom of her pajamas. What was it Quinn had called it? A onesie? "I'm new at this and it'd be great if you'd give me a chance and not cry."

She wiggles, her little hands fisted, swatting at the air, like she's looking to land one on my chin. I take her hand in mine, lean in and give it a kiss. "You're going to be a fighter, aren't you?" I remove her diaper and reach for the baby wipes. "That's good, Daisy. You're so pretty, you're going to have to learn how to fight the boys off."

She makes a noise and gives me a big smile—the first smile I've seen on her—and my heart jumps into my throat. "No way." I turn around, half-expecting Quinn to be there, to witness this moment, but disappointment takes up residency in my gut when I find the room empty. I turn back to Daisy.

"Oh, you like that do you? You want to take care of those boys by yourself." As I look at her, think about who's going to protect my girl once she's in school—a teenager—possession moves through me. Yeah, I know what guys are like, and if any of them think for one moment they're going to get within ten feet of my teenage daughter, they've got another thought coming. I slide the diaper beneath her, tape it up, and re-snap her onesie.

She's cooing and smiling at me when I pick her up and hold her against my chest. "How about we let Quinn sleep a little longer, and I'll get your bottle. We can watch Sportsnet and maybe you can see snippets of your daddy's last game."

Daddy?

Man, will I ever get use to that?

She wiggles in my arms, and her fingers tug at my hair. Damn, I'm going to have to get it cut before she tears it out. We head downstairs, and I take a bottle from the fridge. I set her in her car seat, which is plunked on the kitchen table, and make some coffee, wanting a mug ready for Quinn when she wakes up. My mind races to my best friend's sister.

How will she react this morning?

Will she go running out of here, or take me up on the offer I'm about to make her?

When it comes right down to it, I really shouldn't have seduced her. If she runs now, I'm fucked. Hindsight is a wonderful thing, and now, since neither of us can deny that last night was pretty damn awesome, we can only move forward with that knowledge

The microwave beeps, and as I prepare the bottle, I turn to see Daisy, one of the rubber toys hanging from the car seat handle in her mouth. Heart in my throat, I jump toward her, ready to grab it—but then stop. I guess it's okay for her to chew it. They wouldn't make a car seat toy that wasn't safe, right? Fuck, I have so much to learn.

One day at a time, dude.

As the coffee percolates, I pick her up and we head into the living room. I sit, put the bottle into her mouth and flick on the TV. I go through the stations until I find Sportsnet, showcasing highlights of last night's basketball game. Daisy drinks half her bottle, then I burp her, but before I do, I throw one of her blankets over my shoulder.

Like I said, I'm a quick learner.

Behind me the stairs creak, and Daisy begins to make babbling noises. I angle my head, catch the hesitant look on Quinn's face.

"Sorry if we woke you. I was hoping you'd get more sleep."

"You didn't wake me. I'm always up early. Habit. How is she this morning?" She comes around to face me and tugs on the hem of the T-shirt she's weaning. My T-shirt.

Does she have any panties on underneath?

"Good. I changed her diaper," I say, like a student looking for praise from a teacher. How juvenile is that? Changing the subject, I gesture with a nod toward the kitchen. "Coffee should be done."

"I'll grab us a cup," she says and darts into the other room like wolves are nipping at her heels. Cupboards open and close as she searches for the mugs, and a few minutes later she brings me a much-needed cup.

"Cream, no sugar, right?" she asks.

"You remember," I say, a statement, not a question.

She blows into her cup and sits in the seat across from us. Daisy gives a good burp and I settle her back into my arms, and give her the rest of the bottle.

"You're really good with her, Jonah," she says quietly.

I shake my head. "To think before yesterday I'd never even held a child."

"You really stepped up."

My chest swells. Goddammit, I really like it when she looks at me like that, like she's totally proud of me. Although I don't want to think too hard on why I like it so much.

She goes quiet for a moment, toys with her coffee mug. Is she thinking about last night? Waiting for me to bring it up? I open my mouth, but she speaks first.

"Jonah, about last night..."

I brace myself. "What about it?"

"It was..."

"Fantastic?"

A small smile touches her mouth. "That's one word to describe it, but I'm just not sure—"

"Wait," I say, unable to hear her valid points on why we shouldn't do it again—Christ, I just found out I was a father, and I have an NHL career to think about. Not to mention her brother is going to kill me, and Quinn deserves better than a guy like me, one who has a reputation a mile wide. Plus, she's chasing her own dreams, is building a life for herself that I don't fit into—not that either of us are looking for anything more. We had fun, simple as that.

I lean toward her, Daisy secure in my arms. "You had fun, right?"

She sips her coffee and looks at me over the rim. "I...yes."

"So did I. A lot. So what's a little pleasure between friends? Neither one of us is looking for anything more, so while you're here, helping out, why can't we just keep having sex...enjoy each other?"

She visibly quakes, like she's remembering all the dirty things we did last night, reliving them in her mind's eye. "I..."

I take the empty bottle from Daisy's mouth and put her over my shoulder again. Quinn's face softens as she watches me.

"So you're suggesting we continue to have no-strings sex,

until I find you a nanny?" she asks, and my heart thumps with excitement. At least she's considering it.

"Sure," I say casually, although my stomach is in a chaotic mess. What if she says no? I'm sure fifty hand jobs a night and a harem of puck bunnies would never suffice. Now that I've had a taste of her, I want more. I'm certain by the time we hire a nanny I'll have gotten her out of my system. "And until I find a nanny, I want to pay you for helping out."

She crinkles her nose. "No, I don't want your money," she says adamantly.

Christ, she's so different from the other women I know, which makes me like her all the more. "It's a simple business arrangement, Quinn."

"I can't take your money, Jonah."

"Fine. Then while you're here, I'll pay your half of your father's medical bills."

She sits up a little straighter and her eyes go wide. "How do you know—"

"Your brother is my best friend. We talk. Listen, I get it. You don't want the entire burden to fall on your brother, and that's admirable." Really fucking admirable, considering the women I know what me for one of two things: what's between my legs or what's in my back account. "But what you would have paid, you can save, put it toward that daycare facility you always wanted."

She bites her lip and looks down. "You're not saying no. I won't let you."

"Jonah—"

"Done. It's settled. While you're helping me with Daisy, and helping me find a nanny, I'll pay you."

"You're kind of pushy."

I grin at her. "That's why they call me the Body Checker." She looks down for a moment, and I pray she's not having second thoughts. "What?" I ask.

"Just...I don't think we should tell my brother or anyone else about us."

"Your brother would kick my ass if he knew I was fucking you."

"Since when have you ever been afraid of Zander?"

"He's my best friend, Quinn." Fear niggles at me. I love Zander like a brother, and would never want to hurt him. Goddammit, I should have kept my dick in my pants. "I can't lose him."

She nods, like she understands that. "I know he's overprotective of me, but I'm a big girl, can make my own decisions on who I bring into my bed."

"Then why don't you want anyone to know?" I ask, bluntly.

"I don't want anyone to get the wrong idea, that we might be in a relationship or something. I'm not looking for anything like that."

I take a moment to absorb her words, roll them around in my brain for a second. Would being in a relationship with me be so horrible? Guess so, considering she wants to keep this a secret. Yeah, I know I have a reputation, and she deserves someone better.

Wait, wait. I don't want a relationship either, so what the fuck am I getting all upset about?

Daisy lets loose another burp and Quinn laughs. "Not hard to tell she's your daughter." She shakes her head. "You and Zander were so disgusting, having those burping contests when you were younger."

"I remember you joining in a time or two. If memory serves me correctly, didn't you win after you drank that big glass of root beer?"

She lifts her chin. "I don't remember that at all."

"Yeah right."

"I believe you're having false memories. I would never do

something so disgusting." She stands and stretches out her arms. "Can I hold her for a minute?"

"Way to change the subject," I say, and hand my daughter over.

Quinn smiles as she looks down at little Daisy. "She's so precious."

"You look like you might want one."

Her head rears back. "No."

"Whoa," I say, obviously hitting a sore spot. "Sorry."

"I just...I work at a daycare. When I get home at the end of the night, I want peace and quiet," she says, but I'm not sure I believe. There's something she's not telling me, and I'm not going to push. It's obviously a sensitive subject for her and likely none of my business. "I sent out a few texts to my co-workers yesterday. Hopefully we'll hear something today. Like I said, the sooner we get a nanny, the better."

Okay, okay, I get it. She doesn't want to be here with me longer than necessary. She doesn't have to keep driving the point home. I nod, and just then my cell rings from my bedroom. I glance at the stairs. "Who would be calling me this early in the morning?"

"No clue," Quinn says. "Maybe it's Shari, with a change of heart."

Would I want her taking care of my daughter after pulling a stunt like that?

I hurry up the stairs—and my heart races when I see who the call is from.

I swipe my finger over the phone and head back down to Quinn and Daisy.

"Hi Mom, what are you doing up so early? It's only like six in Mexico, isn't it?"

"What's this we hear about you having a baby?" she says, getting right to the point like she always does.

I meet Quinn's eyes and mouth the words, "My parents. They know."

Quinn cringes. "Wow, news travels fast in the hockey world," she whispers back, as she walks around the room with Daisy, bouncing her gently.

"Is it true?" Mom asks.

"Who have you been talking too?"

"Luke mentioned it to his mother. She called me right away. We all talk you know, and if it is true, why am I not hearing it from my own son?"

"Sorry. I just found out yesterday. She was basically dropped into my arms, and I wanted to figure things out before I called you."

"We're coming home right now."

I pinch the bridge of my nose. Yesterday, I would have been all over the idea, but Daisy isn't my mother's responsibility. She's mine—Quinn beat that fact home—and she shouldn't cut her vacation short because of it.

"No, it's okay. I've got everything under control."

"I hardly think so," she says. "You're not equipped—"

"I know," I say quickly. "But Quinn is here helping. She's going to stay with me for a while, until I can find a nanny."

"Oh," she says, surprise in her voice. "That's awfully generous of her."

"Yes, she's very generous," I say, my gaze on her ass as she sits Daisy in the bassinette we bought yesterday. But suddenly my mind is on other things, like how generous she was with her mouth, her body last night in the kitchen, in bed. Shit. The last thing I want is a boner while I'm talking to my mother.

"Quinn is such a lovely girl. The kind of girl you need in your life, Jonah."

"She *is* in my life, Mom. She's always been in my life."

"You know what I mean. Anyway, who's the mother? Why

did she just leave the child with you? How come she never told you about her before now? Are you even sure she's yours, Jonah?"

"She's mine, Mom."

"Do you plan to marry the girl?"

Jesus, I knew it would lead back to this.

"Listen, just go enjoy your vacation. We'll all talk when you get back, and I'll answer all your questions."

"Are you sure, Jonah? We can catch the next flight and be home by tonight."

"We've got everything under control. I'll fill you in when you get home. Right now, just go and have fun. I insist, Mom," I say, a little more force behind my words.

"Well, if you insist."

"I do. Have fun, tell Dad I said hello, and I'll talk to you later." I slide my finger across the screen to end the call and glance up to find Quinn watching me.

"How did that go?"

"I managed to talk her into not coming home."

"I thought you'd want her here."

"Yesterday I did, but now I have you." I slide my hand around her body and drag her to me. Heat moves into her cheeks. "I'm dying to know, Quinn."

"Know what?" she asks, as I put my hand between her thighs.

"What you're wearing under here," I say, and leisurely slide my hand upward until I find her bare, wet...completely ready for me again.

QUINN

I wake up, roll over and take in the gorgeous, naked man sleeping beside me. His blankets are hovering around his waist, exposing his sexy oblique muscles. My hands itch to touch him, my mouth waters for a taste. I move closer, breathe in his familiar scent, let it stir things inside me. I'm about to touch him but stop myself.

Wait, did I really agree to his terms yesterday? Sex for pleasure while I remain at his house helping? My God, I did. I really did.

And it's a good damn thing, too. I've only been intimate with him two times, and I'm already addicted, not quite ready to give him up. Then again, who could blame me? He's as skilled in the bedroom as he is on the ice. No wonder all the bunnies are tripping over themselves to get a piece of him. But now that he's a father, will that settle him down, or will he go back to his old ways when he's on the road?

I ease from the bed, needing to get ready for work. I'm confident Jonah will be okay alone with Daisy for the day, and I'll be back at dinnertime to give him a break. I'm sure he'll need it by then.

"Where do you think you're going?" Jonah asks, his voice sleepy, groggy.

"I have to work, remember?"

He groans, grabs me and pulls me back to the bed. "Did you really think you were getting out of here without a good-morning kiss?"

A good-morning kiss?

Isn't that what longtime lovers do, kiss one another before they part for the day, and when they arrive home? Since we're not a couple, I hadn't expected to kiss him hello or goodbye.

He climbs over me and, taking me by surprise, he slides down my body and grips the hem of my T-shirt. I'm still in his clothes, despite the fact that I made a trip home yesterday to get my own. But Jonah seems to like me in his shirts for some reason—likely because it gives him easy access to my sex.

He lifts the shirt, and exposes my body.

A grin touches his mouth as he spreads my legs. "Just the way I like you."

I'm about to respond, but he dips his head and widens my lips with his tongue. My words turn into a moan of pleasure, and my hips rise from the bed. "Yes," I murmur, as he presses a hot kiss to my clit. Ah, so this is the good-morning kiss he was talking about. Nothing to do with longtime couples at all. Good, because I don't want that, and I could really get used to waking up like this every morning.

"Mmm," he murmurs as he buries his face between my legs, licking and eating at me, until my body is hot, needy, quaking all over. I reach for him, grip his hair, and move against his invading mouth.

"Jonah," I say, my breath a desperate whisper as he slides a finger into me, then another. He fucks me with both fingers, touching and stroking in all the right places, as his tongue swirls over my clit. My body grows hotter, the room closes in on me. My hands leave his hair, grasp at the bed sheets. I tug, twirl them in my hand as pressure builds. He moans again, loving what he's doing to me, and that knowledge brings on my orgasm. I come and come and come some more, my muscles clenching, a storm of pleasure blowing through me and stealing my breath.

I toss my head from side to side and work to refill my lungs as he continues to kiss me, slower this time, softer, knowing just how to bring me back down. I go up on my elbows to see him, and I'm sure there is no sexier sight than this man between my legs. I shake my head at how quickly he brought me to orgasm. How the hell is he so good at this?

Because he's had a lot of practice.

I wipe that thought from my mind and ignore the unwanted jealousy it provokes.

What's between us is sex. Good sex. Amazing sex. Mind-blowing, orgasmic sex.

My body stops spasming, and he lifts his head, grins up at me, his mouth wet from my release. "Good morning," he says.

"Good morning," I say and try to catch my breath.

He crawls up me, plants his mouth on mine. "Now you can go get ready for work, and while you're there, you can think about all the ways we're going to fuck tonight when you get back." His cock rubs against my leg, hard and ready. He taps the side of my ass. "You better get going. I don't want to make you late."

"What about you?" I ask. He just gave me amazing oral sex; does he not want anything in return?

"Tonight, after we get the baby to bed, you're mine." He touches my breasts. "My mouth needs more time with these. I think I might even fuck you here," he says, running his finger between my cleavage. "Then I'm going to fill your throat with my cum."

I gulp, the image doing crazy things to me, arousing me all over again. "Okay," I squeak out.

He laughs. "I'll probably jack off three times in the shower before that, though."

I laugh with him, but his words thrill me. I've never had a man want me the way this one does.

Don't get too excited about that, Quinn.

Right, right, this is just sex. A secret affair. That might just be the thrill of it for him.

"How do you expect me to work after...this?"

He slides off me and holds his hand out. I take it, and when I stand our bodies collide. "Did you like your good-morning kiss?"

"Ah, yeah," I say, and he laughs.

"Good, be prepared to wake up to that every morning."

"How am I supposed to work today? I can barely freaking walk."

"Just think about all the things we're going to do tonight. It will help get you through the day."

Just then Daisy cries out, and Jonah climbs into his pants as I make a beeline for the shower. I wash quickly, dress, and let my hair dry naturally as I head to the kitchen for a cup of coffee. The sight of Jonah on the sofa with Daisy gives me pause and my heart pinches. It's picture perfect, except for one thing—Daisy doesn't have a mother, and Jonah doesn't have a wife. Not that I want to be either of those things to this ready-made family or become too attached. I'm not about to set myself up for heartache.

Jonah turns his head, and I put on a smile and step toward him.

"Coffee is ready. Do you want me to make you some breakfast? Daisy is just about finished hers."

"No, I'll grab a muffin. I'm running a bit behind."

His grin is evil, and my sex clenches. "Sorry about that but

I couldn't let you leave here without a proper good-morning kiss, now could I?"

"I'll have to set my alarm to wake up a bit earlier."

He chuckles...but then it dies, all humor gone from his face. In its place, exists worry. I sit on the coffee table across from him.

"You okay?"

"Are you sure I can do this?" He puts Daisy over his shoulder, and I touch his leg, give it a comforting squeeze.

"I'm only a phone call away, and so is Zander. He'll help you, Jonah. He knows how to take care of a little girl."

Our eyes meet, lock. "I'm sorry your mom left," he says. "I don't think I ever told you that."

Emotions well up inside me and tears press against the backs of my eyes. "It's okay," I say. "It was a long time ago. Right now, you have Daisy to worry about, not me."

"I just wanted you to know that."

I nod, even though I've always known that. He might not have been able to say the words until now—maybe Daisy brings out a different side of him—but he was always there for Zander, doing things to lighten his burden, like helping him with chores, cooking, cleaning and laundry, which meant he was always there for me, too. Deep down, I knew that.

Maybe I was wrong when I said he cared about no one but himself.

Before I even realize what he's doing, he leans forward and places the softest kiss on my mouth. Our lips linger, no hurried movements, no frenzied tearing of clothes to get each other naked, just a tender exchange that unearths something inside me...something I've kept buried for a long time.

"I'd better go," I say when he pulls back. I stand up quickly and head to the kitchen. I find my phone on the counter and reach for it.

"Jonah," I call out, as I grab my travel mug and fill it with coffee. "Looks like we have a lead on a nanny. I can get the details today and check out her credentials."

"Thanks," he says, but he's standing behind me.

I jump and nearly spill the coffee. "I'm getting you a bell."

He laughs and nods toward my phone. "Keep me posted."

"Yeah, the sooner we can get it arranged, the better. I can't stay on helping forever."

I drop my phone into my purse and look at him—really look at him—and when I do, I suddenly see more than the gorgeous hockey player who is always out to score, on and off the ice.

"You got this, Jonah. I promise."

"You do?" he asks, like my answer is the most important thing he'll ever hear, like it could make or break him.

I touch his arm, then rub Daisy's back. "She's in good hands. I mean that."

"Thank you," he says, and lets loose a breath of relief.

"Okay, I'm off. You know my number, just call or text if you need me."

He walks me to the door, and he turns Daisy in his arm, waving me off with her hand, and my heart jumps into my throat and lodges. I climb into my car and make my way into the city. Forty minutes later, I squeeze my car into my parking spot and head inside.

When I do, I'm bombarded with questions from my co-workers and my best friend, Tina.

"Are you really staying with Jonah Long?" Carrie askes, all wide-eyed and dreamy, like I'm playing house and getting banged by the Body Checker.

"Has the Body Checker checked out your body yet?" Tammy asks.

"It's not like that."

Oh, it's like that. They just don't have to know it.

"Why not?" Tina asks. "If I were you, I'd be tapping that."

I laugh and shake my head. "You're not me. I'm just helping him out."

I turn to Carrie, the daycare director, before Tina can read the lie on my face. I'm just not ready to share the details with anyone, not even my best friend. "This nanny you recommended. Can I get her information?"

"Sure, come on."

"If you start tapping that, I want all the details," Tina says, and I just roll my eyes at her. "Text is fine too," she adds with a laugh.

Carrie sits at her desk and rifles through her papers. "She's my neighbor's daughter. She just received her early childhood education certificate, and wants to start with in-home care."

I take the girl's name and number and drop it into my purse. "Thanks," I say. "I'll be helping Jonah with the interviews, but he has last say, so I can't promise anything."

"Fine by me either way. I can do a little more searching and find you more candidates if you like."

"I'd appreciate that." I'm about to leave when Carrie gives me a strange look. "What?"

"It's good of you to help him like this."

I give a fast wave. "We go way back. He's like my brother," I fib.

Carrie's lips twitch. "Brother? That's how you see him?" she asks, like she can see right through my lie.

Heat burns through me, undoubtedly turning my cheeks a darker shade of pink, so I quickly turn and say, "Yes, that's how I see him," and pray to God my pants don't catch on fire.

I take my phone from my pocket and type Jonah a text, giving him the nanny's name and number, and suggesting he call so we can interview her tonight. My hand lingers over the send button.

Do I really want some girl taking over tonight? That would mean I'm out and she's in.

Would it also mean she'd take over in the bedroom as well? *Send the message already.*

Annoyed with myself, I hit send and put the phone in my back pocket. The sound of laughter reaches my ears, and I go into the playroom to get the activities ready for the kids. They all start to pile in, all bright-eyed and fresh-faced, and ready for their morning playtime.

I'm more tired than usual when lunchtime comes around. Probably because I've been exercising muscles that have been dormant far too long. I head to the lunch room for my break when my phone pings. My heart does a little leap when I see it's Jonah, and I don't want to think too hard on that.

Daisy has a rash. What do I do?

Go to the drugstore and get some cream. Ask the pharmacist what they recommend.

I think we need to get her some more onesies, she's gone through three changes today.

Okay, good idea, I text back.

Do you think it's her formula making her spit up?

I laugh. *No, she's just a baby. Babies spit up.*

I'll talk to the pharmacist, ask about that.

Okay, talk to you later.

What time do you think you'll be home?

Around five-thirty.

I'll try to have dinner ready.

No worries, you have your hands full.

She's been crying a lot today. Maybe she misses you. Oh, I was going to give her a bath, Google said that would help, but I don't want to do that without you.

We'll do that tonight.

I stare at the phone, and three dots keep repeating. I wait for Jonah's next text to come through but it doesn't. Whatever he was going to say, he must have changed his mind. I'm about to put my phone back in my pocket but consider texting Zander to check up on Jonah. Then change my mind. I don't want him to think I called in reinforcement because he can't handle a four-month-old.

The rest of the day passes quickly, as it always does in the daycare, and after seeing all the kids off to their waiting parents, Carrie meets me at the door with a list of names.

"Wow, you really came through for me. Thank you."

"I made a few calls. No problem at all. I hope you find someone to care for the child." A pause, and then, "I know it's not my business but where is her mother?"

"We don't know, she just dropped the baby off."

"Do you think she'll come back for her?"

I give that thought more consideration. Would it break Jonah's heart to hand his daughter over, or will he be relieved? I can already see the bond growing, but hockey is his first love. Would he grow to resent Daisy? The responsibility of taking care of a child has already interfered with his lifestyle, and worrying about her when he's on the road could interfere with his game. He might be stepping up, but this isn't what he wants. Not really.

"I'm not sure what's going to happen. Right now, we're just trying to get by day by day."

Carrie puts her hand on my shoulder. "Just be careful, okay?"

Careful?

Why would she tell me to be careful? I'm about to ask, when a car horn sounds and Carrie waves. "That's Dave. Gotta run." She leaves the center, and once the place is empty, I grab my purse, lock up, and head home.

Home?

Well, not my home, but Jonah's home. I crack the window and let the warm breeze fall over me as I drive. When I reach

Jonah's place, his car isn't in the driveway. Although it could be in the garage.

I park and walk up to the front door to find it locked. Unease worms through me, and I knock. Could they be inside sleeping? If so, I don't want to wake them up. Then again, maybe he's at the drugstore. I spin around and shade the late-day sun from my eyes as I figure out my next move. Should I call Zander? He has a key to the place. I pull out my phone, and I'm about to dial when Jonah's car comes down the road at a snail's pace.

I hurry down the stairs and meet them in the driveway. "Everything okay?" I say, working to keep my voice casual as I glance into the backseat, seeing a sleeping baby.

Jonah climbs out looking ragged and unkempt, with his hair a mess and food stains on his shirt. I've never seen him like this, but he looks so damn adorable. Wait, is that dried milk in his hair?

"She was exhausted, and I couldn't get her to sleep," he explains.

I grin. "So you took her for a ride."

"Yeah, I googled it." He opens the backseat and unhooks the baby seat, keeping Daisy in it.

"Did you get the cream for her rash?"

"Yeah, and do you think Pampers or Huggies are better? I wasn't sure and was going to text you, but decided to buy both." He pops the trunk to reveal two big boxes. I grab them and follow him up the steps. He unlocks the door and carries Daisy in, then turns to me. "I had this made for you today." He hands me a key to his place. "If you're going to be staying here, you need your own key."

I drop the diapers and close my hand around the shiny new key. "Good plan," I say. Then tease, "Are you sure about this, Jonah? If I can come and go as I please, I might catch you with one of your girlfriends."

"You're the only girl in my life, Quinn," he states flatly. Then he glances at his sleeping daughter. "Well, you and Daisy." My stupid heart twists at that, then I give myself a good hard lecture.

You don't want to be his girl, Quinn.

I follow him into the kitchen, take in the mess. He gives me a sheepish look, and it's so damn adorable, I want to take him into my arms and hug him.

"I'm sorry," he says quickly. "I know you told me to keep the place clean, but Daisy is quite the handful."

I truly love how hard he's trying. "It's bottles and toys and clothes, Jonah. Not beer bottles and empty pizza boxes."

"Speaking of pizza boxes. Do you want to order something in?"

Daisy fusses in her seat, and Jonah releases the straps and holds her to him. She instantly settles—and that's when I think about Carrie's warning. What *will* happen if the mother comes back? It's definitely something Jonah has to consider and be prepared for.

"I didn't have time to cook for you. This little one is a full-time job."

"I can make us something," I say. "We had groceries delivered." I pull open the fridge. "How about BBQ hamburgers and salad?"

"Works for me."

He bounces with Daisy in his arms, and I pull all the ingredients from the fridge. "Did you call about the nanny?" I ask.

"She'll be here tonight around seven."

A pang of disappointment settles in my gut. "That's great, and if she doesn't work out, I have a whole list of names for you. Recommended by the daycare director."

We step outside and the warm air falls over me. I glance

at the big pool in the backyard. "You're going to have to babyproof that, Jonah," I say as I light the grill.

"I've been thinking the same thing. I have to babyproof the whole house."

I nod, but then say, "We should wait on that." In the back of my mind, I can't help but think Shari is going to show up and reclaim her daughter. Then again, Jonah will likely want visitation rights, and his house will have to be ready for that.

Jonah goes to the pool and sits, dangling his legs in the water. I toss the meat onto the grill, baste it, and then join him. I hike my pants up and dip my feet in.

"That feels glorious."

"Why don't we have a swim later?" he says, but there is mischief in his eyes. Warm need moves through me, and when his thigh brushes mine, my thoughts go off in a million directions. With my body growing needy, I stand, flip the burgers and hurry inside to whip up a salad. I glance out the window, and Daisy is now awake. Jonah is lifting her over his head and she's grinning at him. My heart wobbles at the cuteness.

"Quinn," he calls out, and I run outside. "I think she likes me," he says, the childlike enthusiasm in his voice making me laugh.

"I told you it would just take time."

He winks at me. "I'm used to women liking me sooner than that. Well, except for you. It took you ten years to like me."

Oh, if he only knew.

He holds Daisy up again and she breaks out in a big smile.

"Careful, Jonah," I warn. "You're holding her over your face, and she's a wet burper."

"Oh, Jesus," he says and puts her back on his lap. We both laugh, and I point at him.

"Language."

"Shit, right." He climbs from the edge of the pool. "Can we help you with anything?"

"Why don't you set the table, things are just about ready."

He sets Daisy in her car seat and she plays with the rubber rings, her big blue eyes bright and shiny, like she had a good day with Jonah. My heart warms at that as I load the plates with our burgers and salad. I carry them to the table, and Jonah is about to sit across from me when his phone pings. He hesitates, like he's not sure whether to answer it or not.

"You'd better get it," I say. "It could be about Daisy."

He looks at the caller and frowns, and my heart jumps. Is it Shari, wanting to come back for her daughter? Jonah scratches his head, then slides his finger across his phone.

"Hey Katee," he says, and our eyes meet. "No, no, I'm fine. Really."

I sit there and try not to listen to his conversation, but it's impossible.

"Quinn is here." A pause, and then, "That's right, Zander's sister. She's a daycare teacher. She's helping me." He picks up his fork and toys with it, an uncomfortable look on his face. "Katee, I'm fine. You don't need to come here."

I take a drink of my water, and when he's finally able to get her off the phone, he looks at me.

"Sorry about that."

"Everything okay?" I ask as he sits across from me.

"Yeah, that was Katee. News certainly spreads fast. My phone has been pinging since Saturday morning, lots of offers to help."

"How nice that she wants to help you out," I say, and stab my cucumber, hating—absolutely hating—the jealousy rising up inside me. "Maybe you should take her up on that."

"Why would I take her up on that when I have you?"

"Not for long," I say, and my stomach clenches. I've only

been here for three days, and I'm already growing to like every moment with these two.

"I know, you keep reminding me," he says, then he picks up his knife and redirects. "I usually eat at the island," he says, and we both glance at the marble countertop, to the spot where he pleasured me. My thighs quiver at the memories, and our gazes meet. He shakes his head, like he's shocked at the turn his life has taken. "Then again, I'm doing a lot of things I've never done before." He looks down at his food, his mood changing. "I have to say, I'm a little scared, Quinn," he admits honestly, and my heart goes out to him.

He's not the only one who's scared. When I see him holding his baby, making her smile, it draws me in a little deeper, has me thinking about my future...one where kids and a husband *do* exist. Only problem is, when I visualize that little scenario, both Daisy and Jonah figure prominently.

9

JONAH

I listen to Quinn talk to 'baby talk' to Daisy, as I load the dishwasher and clean the kitchen. Her sweet whispered words bring a smile to my face, but they also make me wonder why she's so adamant that she doesn't want a family of her own. Zander is the opposite. Sure, he's young and playing the field right now, but he talks about settling down in the future. I can see him with a kid. He'd make a great dad. Way better than me, that's for sure.

I turn the dishwasher on and head into the living room to find my girls playing on the sofa.

My girls?

Well, for the time being, they're both mine. Just then, the doorbell rings.

"Must be the nanny," Quinn says as she bundles Daisy up and holds her to her chest in a protective manner.

I make my way to the door, and when I pull it open, there is a young girl standing on my stoop, an envelope in her hand. Her eyes go wide when they see me. Well, not me, but the Body Checker.

"You're...you're..."

"Jonah Long," I say, and step back to wave her in.

She curls a strand of hair around her finger and steps into the room, and her eyes land on Quinn and the baby. Quinn steps up to her and introduces the baby, then herself.

"I'm Rebecca," she says, and hands me the envelop. She looks young, like high-school young. "Here's my resume."

"Why don't you have a seat," Quinn says. "Can I get you anything to drink?"

"No, I'm good thanks," she says as her nervous glance moves to me again. I pull the paper from the envelope and look it over quickly. After high school, she did a two-year certification course. On paper, she seems to have everything one would need to care for a child, but I worry about her experience.

Quinn and I sit on the sofa together, a united team—outside the bedroom, for once in our lives—and face Rebecca, who folds her hands and places them on her thighs.

"Can you tell us a little about yourself?" Quinn asks.

"I received my certification last month, and I'm looking forward to starting in-house care. Eventually I want to open my own daycare."

Quinn smiles at her. "Do you have any experience?"

"I have three younger brothers," she says and laughs. "Plus, I used to babysit through high school." She points to her resume. "I have references."

"Is there anything you'd like to ask us?" I say.

"Would I have my weekends off?"

Both Quinn and I exchange a fast look, then I say, "When I'm on the road, I need someone here caring for Daisy full time."

"Oh, I didn't realize." She frowns and looks down for a second.

"Will that be a problem for you?" I ask.

Her eyes lift. "No. Not at all," she says, and glances around the room. "You guys have a lovely home."

"Oh, we're just friends," Quinn says. "I'm helping him out until he finds a nanny."

"Oh," she says, her eyes wide. "You're not the baby's mother?"

Quinn, as though realizing just how tight she'd been holding Daisy, hands her over to me. "No. I'm just a friend. Jonah and I go way back."

"Her mother currently isn't in the picture," I add.

"Oh, that's too bad. Poor little girl needs a mother figure." She scoots forward on her chair. "Well, I hope you give my application consideration. I would love to work for you, Jonah. I'm also a great cook. I'm good at many things."

Beside me, Quinn stiffens, and I give a curt nod. "We'll definitely consider it," I say, and stand. Rebecca stands with me, and I walk her to the door, Daisy in my arms.

She gives a little wave as she leaves, and tells me she'll be looking forward to a call. I close the door, lean against it, and shake my head at Quinn, who has a worried look on her face.

"No way," I say, and she blows out a breath. "Not in a million years."

Quinn throws her head back, rests it on the cushion and stares at the ceiling. "Thank God."

"She never even once looked at Daisy, or asked about her," I say.

"Once she saw you, I think she went brain dead."

I laugh at that. "Star-struck. It happens."

"If that's what you want to call it. If I wasn't here, I'm sure she would have handed you her panties."

With Daisy asleep in my arms, I move to set her in the bassinette. "Yeah, but your panties are the only ones I want," I say, my mind shifting.

"I think you have that wrong. You don't want me in

panties, remember? I'm not even sure what you did with the ones you stripped off me the other day."

"Maybe I'm keeping them."

"I didn't know cross-dressing was another one of your things." Standing up, she holds her hands up, palms out. "Hey, I'm not judging. To each their own, right?"

I can't help but grin at her. "That's right, to each their own, which brings me back to this morning. Do you remember what I said to you this morning, what else was my...thing?"

She gulps, and I step up to her, pull her against my body. "I believe you said something about my mouth."

I laugh. "Can't say it?"

"Oh, I can say it," she says with a lift of her chin. "I can say a lot of things. I just don't want to do it in front of the baby."

"How about we put the baby to bed?"

"We need to bathe her, remember."

"Shit, right." I remove Daisy from the bassinette. "But don't think this gets you off the hook. Later, you're going to talk dirty to me."

She laughs and rushes up the stairs. When I get to the top, she's in the bathroom, running water. I follow her in, and she has her hand in the stream, testing it. "Can you run into her room and get her little bath tub?"

I go to her room, grab the pink tub and carry it back. "So much pink," I say.

"Get used to it. You've got a little girl."

"Do you think I should paint her room? Make it more girly for her?"

"Yeah, and if you like, I could help. I would love to decorate her room. I mean, if Zander is her uncle, that makes me her aunt, right?"

"Yeah, I guess I never looked at it like that, Aunty Quinn."

Working as a team, Quinn fills the tub, and I sit on the edge of it and undress a sleeping Daisy. My big fingers work the snaps, and I carefully pull the onesie over her head. She fusses a bit, but then settles. Little wisps of hair lift from the static, and I run my hand over them.

"I think she's going to be blonde like you."

"That's just baby hair. She'll probably have dark hair like you." She tests the water again. "You can set her in."

I go to my knees on the floor and carefully lift Daisy over the edge of the tub. Her arms go out wide, and her lids open, but only briefly, because once Quinn starts sprinkling her with warm water, she falls back to sleep and I swear to God she's smiling.

Quinn unwraps the soap and starts lathering up a cloth. She hands it to me.

"I don't know what to do."

She chuckles softly. "You wash yourself, don't you?"

"Yeah, but…"

"Like this," she says, and takes my hand. She keeps hers over mine as we both lightly run the suds over the baby. "Be sure to get in the crevices," she says, lifting the baby's arm to clean all the pudgy spots.

"You're so good with her, Quinn," I say. We touch a little more intimately now, our hands twined as we clean my daughter.

After we soap her up, we rinse her with clean water, and Quinn pours a pea-size drop of baby shampoo into her palm.

"We wash her hair?" I ask.

"Of course."

"But she hardly has any."

"Doesn't matter." She brings the shampoo to my nose.

"Doesn't this smell good. I always loved the smell of baby soaps and shampoos."

I inhale. "Yeah, nice."

Together we wash her hair, and I hold a cloth over her eyes to keep the shampoo out. Once we're done, and she's all clean, I wrap her in a towel and carry her into the bedroom. Quinn sets a diaper on the changing table and grabs her a clean onesie.

"She does have a little rash, doesn't she," Quinn says as I rub cream onto her sore spots. "Don't worry though, it's normal."

I fix her diaper, dress her and hold her a minute longer, breathing in her soapy scent. "I didn't think getting a nanny was going to be so hard."

"Maybe the next one should be in her sixties, so she's not all infatuated with you."

"I guess you were hoping it would work out with Rebecca?"

She shrugs. "I want the right person for Daisy. I *am* her aunt."

"I'm sorry you have to stay longer. I promise to make it worth your while."

"You already have," she says, and then pinches her lips shut, like she said too much.

"Yeah?" I push. "Exactly how have I made it worth your while?"

"Not in front of the child," she says, and saunters out of the room, an extra wiggle to her sweet ass.

I set Daisy in her crib and wait a second. Once she settles in, I lean down and give her a kiss on the cheek, then leave to find Quinn standing outside in the hall, waiting for me. Exhaustion pulls at me, and I stretch my arms over my head. "It's been a day," I say.

"Oh, you think it's over?" Quinn asks, teasing me.

I step into her and our bodies bump. "Something on your mind? Something you'd like to show me?"

"Daisy isn't the only one I have to bathe tonight." She reaches out and pulls at the dried milk caked to my hair. "You're a bit of a hot mess, Jonah."

"Why don't you clean me up then." I tap her ass, and lead her to my master bedroom, with the master bath built for two.

I turn on the shower to let the water warm up, and when I turn back to Quinn, she's brushing her tongue over her lower lip, and my cock thickens. "You are so goddamn sexy, Quinn."

A smile touches her mouth. "You're not so bad yourself," she says, and puts her hands on my chest. Her fingers splay, caress my chest, then shoulders, before her hands move to the hem of my shirt. She grips it and pulls it up. I help her remove it and toss it onto the floor.

She steps around me, running her soft hands all over me. I go still, let her explore my body, let her have her way. For now. She stops and presses hot kisses to my back as her hands snake around the front of my sides. Her fingers work the button on my jeans, and the hiss of the zipper cuts through the quiet. She slides her hand in, captures my swollen cock.

"Mmm," she moans into my ear, and I nearly shoot off in her hand.

"Find something you like?" I ask.

"I believe I did," she says, and my head falls back as she strokes me, using the pre-cum as lubricant.

"That feels so fucking good, Quinn."

"I bet I can make it feel even better."

She removes her hand, and I turn to face her. Her fingers go to her blouse, and she slowly unbuttons it. I'm so goddamn anxious to get my mouth on her, if she doesn't hurry, I'm going to tear her shirt off.

"Something wrong?" she asks, as I scrub my hand over my chin, the other going to my throbbing dick.

"Yeah, I need you naked. Now."

"These buttons," she says. "There so tiny."

"Do you like that shirt, Quinn?"

"I like it well enough." She works at one button, can't seem to get it through the hole.

"Is it replaceable?"

Her eyes go wide, like she knows exactly what's pinging around inside my brain. "Yes," she whispers.

I step up to her, back her into the wall, and put her hands over her head. "Keep them there."

Her pulse jumps at the base of her throat as I grip the shirt and tear it open, the little buttons clattering on the tile floor. Her gasp curls around me as I grip her bra and pull it down to expose her pale pink nipples. "These," I say. "I need my mouth on these." I lean into her and roughly pull one nub into my mouth, kissing it, rolling my tongue over it, and clamping down with my teeth.

"Jonah," she cries out, her entire body quaking.

"Mmm," I say, and suck on her other nipple, giving it the same torturous treatment, until Quinn is a quivering mess of need and pleasure.

I stand back, look at the love bruises I gave her and smile. I like branding her. Like seeing my marks on her skin. But that thought brings on another, one that fills me with possession.

"While you're here with me, helping out, you're mine, Quinn. No one else's, okay?" She stares at me, her big blue eyes wide and filled with lust. "Okay?" I ask again, a little more force behind that one word, as I think about another man's hands on her body. No way. No fucking way do I like the image, or the rage it arouses in me.

Careful dude, this is just sex.

She nods. "And you?" she asks.

"I don't want anyone else but you," I say, my body so damn hard and needy for her, I'm not sure I'm thinking straight. "I only want *you* in my bed."

Fuck, it's true. I only want her in my bed. I just pray to fuck when we find a nanny, I'll have gotten her out of my system. There is no future for us, right? Jesus, she doesn't even want anyone to know she's sleeping with me, to get the wrong idea about us, and her brother would fucking kill me.

Her entire body softens, and I sense a change in her as she opens to me, offering herself up completely. "There is nowhere else I'd rather be than in your bed." Her hands slide down the wall, and she unzips her skirt, wiggling it down her legs. "But why don't we start in the shower."

Jesus, she's fucking killing me.

I stand back and take pleasure in her beautiful naked body as she undresses. I keep my hand on my dick, stroking softly, and from the way she's watching me, making soft, sexy noise, I get that she likes it. Who knew this woman would be so playful, so open and uninhibited in the bedroom? I have to say I love this side of her.

I kick off my pants, and when she steps into the steam and crooks her finger, I follow her in. The hot spray feels good on my body, but Quinn feels even better in my hands. She grabs my soap and runs it over my tight muscles.

"That feels good," I murmur, but she had her fun, now it's my turn.

I take the soap from her, lather my hands, and start at her shoulders. Eager to touch every inch of her body—and I mean every inch—I scrub the workday from her flesh. I run my hand over her arms, breasts and stomach. She stands there, eyes closed, a slight smile on her mouth. I shift her, pulling her under the spray to rinse the bubbles, then I turn her around. I move her hair from her shoulders and run my hands over her back and sides. Testing her, I lean her forward and brace her hands on the wall, until her sweet ass is aimed my way.

I soap my hands again, grab her soft cheeks and knead them like dough. I slide one finger between her crevice, and move it slowly around her puckered opening, teasing it open. Her breathing changes, a little hitch in her voice when she gasps, which speaks volumes. She's never been touched like this before. My chest puffs up, thrilled that I'm the first. I apply a tiny bit of pressure to her opening, taking extra care of her body, wanting to do this right for her, as I slide my other hand around her hips to stroke her clit.

"Jonah," she whispers, and starts to move against me. Every time she rears back, my finger goes a little deeper into her sweet ass, but I'm careful not to give her too much her first time. I reposition, move to her side, so I can dip a finger into her hot little pussy and rub by palm over her clit. She moves faster, riding both of my fingers at the same time.

"That's it, Quinn. Fuck my fingers, take what you need."

A moan rolls out of her throat, and her clit swells beneath my ministrations. She's so wet, her desire is dripping down my hand. I fucking love seeing her like this, love that I can do this for her. I kiss her shoulder, nip at it, and she moves a little quicker, a frantic grind of her hips as an orgasm pulls at her.

"When I get you on my bed, I'm going to eat your sweet cunt, and make you come and come and come again, so hard that I'm still going to taste you on my tongue a week from now."

"Jonah, yes," she says.

"Then I'm going to put you on your knees and feed you my cock. I want you to swallow all my cum, Quinn. Every fucking drop. For the next week, every times you swallow, it will remind you of me, because I don't want anyone but me, and how we fuck, in your thoughts."

Her fingers curl on the tile wall, and her pussy muscles swell then clench tightly around my fingers. My dick throbs, wanting to feel that sweet pressure, but that will have to wait. Her wet desire spills from her body, each clench of her muscles drawing my finger in deeper and deeper. I twirl my finger in her backside to increase the sensations of her release and she cries out my name. I've never heard anything sweeter.

I pull my fingers from her body and hold her to me, until she finds the strength to stand on her own after that powerful orgasm. I bring her back under the spray, and she wipes her wet hair from her face and looks up at me.

"I never..."

My heart thuds as she blinks. Honest to God, I've never seen her look more beautiful. "I know," I say, and bend to give her a soft kiss. Her lips part, and I have to say, I love how every inch of her body opens for me.

"It felt...different."

"Different good, or different bad?" I ask.

"Kind of weird," she says, and I laugh.

"What is it with you and weird?" I ask as her hand goes to my dick. "Fuck, yeah," I murmur.

"I like weird with you, Jonah," she says. "I like the way you touch me. I'm not sure I ever would have let another guy do that to me, but I..."

My heart misses a beat. "You what?"

"I trust you."

I cup her face, and don't take her words lightly. "I'd never do anything to hurt you, Quinn."

"Well, there was that one time I fell from the tree because of your dare."

"Do you have any idea how much I hated myself for that?

How much I beat myself up for it? I even asked Zander to punch me in the face, but he wouldn't."

She chuckles and presses her mouth to my chest. She licks me lightly, trailing her tongue over my nipple. "You're crazy."

"I know."

"I like fucking you, Jonah," she says, catching me by surprise. "Sex, it was…never like this before. I'm not that experienced."

Equal amounts of anger and joy curl through me. I'm angry that no man has done sex right for her before, but I'm happy that I'm the first who's made it great.

I touch her chin, lift it until our eyes meet. "I'm sorry," I say—and wonder how I'm going to let her go once we find a nanny.

"I never really loved giving oral sex before, wasn't sure I was very good at it," she says honestly. "But I really like your cock in my mouth."

I groan as the visual hits me.

"Speaking of that," she says, "Didn't you say something about putting me on my knees and fucking my mouth?"

"Fuck, Quinn. I had no idea that you were into talking dirty."

"Neither did I."

That gives me pause. "What?"

She cocks her head to the side and rounds her finger over my nipple as she widens her legs, and presses her sweet pussy against my thigh. She begins to rub her hot sex against me, and I can hardly fucking believe how much her shameless need is turning me on. "I think you bring that out in me," she murmurs.

I reach past her and turn off the shower. "I need to fuck you. Now." I grab a towel, dry her body, then wrap her in it. I knot another towel around my waist, and carry her into my bedroom.

I set her down and run my thumb over her lips. She opens her mouth, draws it in and sucks on it.

"You're so fucking good with your mouth, babe," I say, and her eyes go wide. "What, did you think you weren't?" I pull my thumb out so she can talk.

"I think I'm only good at it with you because I like doing it."

Jesus, I love her all open and honest with me like this. It shouldn't surprise me, really. She's not a girl who holds her punches.

"Well, that's good, because I *like* you doing it," I say, and unknot her towel so it falls to the floor and exposes her beautiful body. She glances down at my cock, which is peeking out from the towel. With a soft touch, she lightly brushes my crown, and my body tightens.

"I want all your cum," she says. "Every drop." With that, she sinks to her knees and removes my towel.

"Fuck, Quinn." I grip her hair and tug on it slightly, so her mouth opens. Her eyes light up as she glances at me. She widens her mouth even more, and I slide my cock in. Her hot mouth closes around me, and I'm sure I found heaven.

My moan of pleasure mingles with hers, and to know she loves what she's doing turns me on even more. I move my hips, slide my cock in and out of her mouth. I want to get deeper, want my cock all the way down her throat—*need* it down her throat for some fucking reason—but I don't want to choke her. This is Quinn. She deserves to be handled right.

Gathering all my restraint, I inch out, and she grips my hips to hold me. I rock into her, and she gives a frustrated moan as she glances up at me.

"Quinn?" I ask.

She goes back on her heel. "I want it hard and rough, Jonah. I'm a big girl. I can take it. Now give me your cock and don't hold back."

Holy fuck.

Her mouth goes back to my dick, and I grip her hair tighter. I push into her, hit the back of her throat and then some. I moan, and it seems to encourage her. She takes me deeper than I've ever been taken before, and a need tears through me.

"You want it like this, Quinn? You want my cock all the way in your mouth, so I can fill your throat with my cum?"

She makes a whimpering sound as I pull out slightly, but I cut off her moan as I drive back in, impossibly deep. I fuck her mouth, and it's never, ever been this good for me before, and no fucking way will it ever be this good again, unless it's with Quinn. What is it about her that makes sex a million times better?

I move my hips, plunder her mouth, frantic, blunt thrusts that take me to the edge fast. She reaches between my legs, grabs my sac, and when her heat seeps into my balls, I lose it. I hold her head still and spurt into her mouth. She swallows and swallows and swallow, but the sex was so good, my load is too big, and some spills out of her mouth.

When I stop coming, I drop to my knees, panting for air. Cum dribbles down her chin as she licks her lips, and I use my thumb to scoop it up and feed it to her.

"Mmm," she murmurs, and I just kneel there and look at her, incredulous.

"You are fucking amazing," I say, and with her eyes closed, like she's savoring the taste of me, she just smiles. "I love fucking you, too. I'm not sure I said that earlier."

"You didn't say it," she says. "But you showed me."

I laugh at that. "Yeah, I guess I did, and after I get you a drink of water, I'm going to show you again and again."

QUINN

I roll over in my bed—I mean Jonah's bed—and check the time. I grin when I see it's almost nine o'clock, and Daisy is still asleep in her room. Over the last week, we've really been working hard on her routine, and even though it's the last thing I want, that little girl is weaving her way into my heart. Could that be why none of the nannies we interviewed over the week didn't make the cut, always came up short? Truthfully, some of them came with high credentials, and really seemed to love Daisy. Sooner or later we're going to have to decide. Only problem is, I want it to be later, despite the fact that it should be sooner. My heart might not be able to handle too much more of this.

I flop back down on the bed, thankful it's Saturday and I don't have to rush off to work. Although I must say, I have been looking forward to the mornings, and the intimate kisses Jonah gives me to wake me up. I roll toward him, and he's on his back, hand over his forehead, still asleep. As I take in his beautiful body, a wicked idea forms. Maybe I'll give him the good-morning kiss this time.

I move quietly and position myself between his legs. His

cock is half hard. What the hell is he dreaming about? A part of me—a really big part—hopes it's me. I mentally scold myself for that thought. While I'm here we're exclusive, but when it's over, it's over, and he can dream about any woman he likes. I shake off the horrible way that makes me feel and lean into him, taking his cock into my mouth the way he likes.

I suck on him, give long, leisurely licks, and he thickens before my eyes. I glance at him. He's up on his elbows and the grin on his face makes my heart wobble.

"Good morning," I say, and his smile widens.

"Great morning."

I lick his crown. "I thought it was my turn to treat you."

"Treat me all you want, but don't think you're getting out of this bed before I bury my face in you pussy."

My entire body quivers. I love the way he wants me. He touches my face, and I take him to the back of my throat. We've been having sex all week. You'd think we'd be worn out, tired of each other, but all this sex has turned me into a nymphomaniac and has me craving more. How I'm going to go back to the dating scene after this is beyond me.

"Mmm," I moan around his thick cock, and he shifts, his fingers tucking my hair behind my ear, so he can get a good look. I put on a show for him, and my head bobs as I fuck him with my mouth, savoring his tang.

"That is so fucking good, babe," he says, his voice an octave deeper. "I could get used to waking up like this on the weekends."

I grip his length, stroke him and slide my mouth lower to suckle his balls, wanting to make this good-morning wake up as great as he's been making them for me all week.

"Motherfucker," he growls, and I grin, loving that I can take this big hockey player to his knees in the bedroom. I stroke faster, the way he likes, and he flops down on the bed, grips the pillow with his hands and drags it halfway over his face. His muscles tighten, ripple, and the second I take his crown back into my mouth, he spurts down my throat. I stay between his legs longer, drink every last drop of him, then lick him clean.

I go back on my knees, and his breathing is harsh. A damp sheen of moisture covers his skin. The look of a well-fucked guy.

"Get up here," he says, and I lay over him, climb up his body. "Not like that." He grips my hips. "Legs around my chest." When I realize what he wants me to do, my sex quivers in anticipation. I spread my legs around his thick chest and he shimmies lower, positioning his mouth under my pussy. "Ride my tongue," he says.

I grab my breasts, pinch my nipples and move my hips. His tongue slashes against my clit in the most glorious ways, and I lean forward, grip the headboard and grind down on him. He shoves his tongue inside me as I work my clit over his face. My body heats up and my blood burns as wild and wicked sensations zing through me, center on the needy juncture between my legs.

"Jonah," I murmur, my orgasm so close, it's all I can do to hang on. He grips my ass, squeezes my cheeks, and clamps down on my clit as he lightly presses a finger into my back passage. Lust rips through me, and while I don't want this to end, my body surrenders, giving in to the intense pleasure. I come all over his mouth, and he moans, rubs his face all around my sopping wet pussy, and keeps me there until he's had his fill.

My legs are trembling by the time he slides me down his body, my hot sex wide open against his stomach.

I shake my head as I look at him. "Sex with you is insane," I say, and he laughs.

"I love eating your pussy, Quinn. I love tasting you on my tongue all day long."

I plant one hand on my hip. "Well, it's awfully nice of me to let you do that every morning, don't you think?"

He laughs harder, and I put my hand over his mouth. "Shh, don't wake the baby."

He cringes. "Right," he whispers—but as soon as the word leaves his mouth, someone unlocks the front door downstairs, and footsteps echo through the house.

"Who could that be?" I ask, my heart racing a little faster.

"Other than you, Zander is the only one with a key."

Stairs creak as Zander comes up them.

"Shit." I jump from the bed and dart into the bathroom. Jonah and I look like we just had a sex marathon. Zander can't see us like this.

I close the bathroom door, just as my brother knocks on Jonah's. "You awake, buddy?"

"Yeah, just getting up," Jonah says. "I'll be right down."

"I'll check on Quinn."

Oh. Shit. No.

Daisy lets out a loud wail.

"Why don't you go check on Daisy for me. I'm sure she'd be happy to see her uncle. She seems to like you better than me anyway."

"Yeah, okay," he says and chuckles.

Thank you, Daisy!

I listen to Zander talk quietly to the baby, and I peek out the bathroom door in time to see Jonah pull on a pair of jeans before meeting Zander in Daisy's room.

"Let's let Quinn sleep," Jonah says. "She was up half the night."

I put my hand over my mouth and stop a moan, as I think about the real reason I was up half the night, not the one he's alluding to.

The three go downstairs and I dart back to my room. I look at my bed, one I only spent one night in, since I agreed to Jonah's proposal. I shake my head. Honesty, what the hell am I doing playing house here? I'm getting in deep with this family. The one thing I swore I couldn't do.

I grab some clean clothes and head to the bathroom for a quick shower. The last thing I want is to greet Zander with sex written all over me. I wash quickly, pull on a sundress, and pass Daisy's room, glancing in. We'd picked out some paint, but we've been too busy to get it done. My gaze goes to the rocking chair. The room is going to be lovely for Daisy once it's done.

I head down to say hello. Zander smiles when he sees me, but then he frowns, a change coming over him. Goddammit, does he know? I'm pretty sure he wouldn't like the idea of me in bed with his best friend. Guilt niggles at me. I don't like hiding things from my brother, and when it comes right down to it, I'm a grown woman, can sleep with anyone I want. Still, Zander might not see it that way, and I owe his so much.

"Zander," I say and give him a hug. "What are you doing here today?"

"Wanted to check up on my little family."

My heart jumps into my throat. "What do you mean?"

He gives me a look that suggests I'm dense. "My sister, niece and best friend." Once again, he's looking at me strangely, then he turns his focus to Jonah, who's averting his gaze, staring at his daughter—an excuse not to meet his best friend's eyes.

"It's good to see you two haven't killed each other yet," Zander comments.

"Daisy is my focus," I say.

Zander turns to the baby gobbling her bottle. "How is she?"

"She's doing great. We have a good routine for her, and she's thriving."

"I was going to get Dad today, take him to the park. Why don't you guys join us? I'm sure he'd love to meet Daisy." He laughs. "He's tired of waiting for us to give him grandkids. He'll have to settle for Jonah's child."

My gaze slides to Jonah, and he nods like it's a brilliant idea.

"I think we could all use some fresh air," I say, considering the amount of time we've been spending in bed.

"Anything from Shari?" he asks, and tentatively looks at me.

"Nothing," Jonah says. "Have *you* heard anything? Anyone talking about where she might be?"

"She has family in Georgia. That's all I heard. Do you want me to try to get a number for you?"

Jonah goes quiet for a moment. "She just left her, Zander. I'm not sure I ever want to speak to her again. But on the other hand, she's Daisy's mother." Jonah's head lifts slowly, his eyes locked on mine. "A little girl should never grow up without her mother," he says quietly, and my throat tightens. His gaze slides to Zander. "No one should."

"Just let me know what you want to do. What about a nanny? Find anyone yet?"

"You're full of questions this morning," I say.

"We interviewed quite a few candidates last week. We're still searching. Not sure any of them were suitable, though."

"That's because you got the best girl right here," Zander says and pulls me to him. He rubs his knuckles along my skull like he used to do when we were kids.

"Cut it out," I say, and pinch his side, like *I* always used to do, but he holds me a little longer and the guys laugh. I struggle to get free, and whack his arm when I finally do.

"I'm not twelve anymore, you know." I smooth my hair down.

"You'll always be twelve to me, kid."

I fold my arms and glare at my brother, but I get that he's just protective.

Zander checks his watch. "Okay, so I'll go pick up Dad and meet you guys in say, an hour?"

I glance at the clock. "Sounds about right."

He pushes from the chair and I follow him to the door. After he leaves, I let loose a breath. "That was a close one, Jonah."

"Too close. Maybe I should change the locks."

"Oh, like that's not going to raise his suspicions." He puts Daisy over his shoulder and burps her. "Want me to finish with her while you shower?"

He hesitates, like he doesn't want to put too much responsibility on me. I hold my hands out. "If we want to be out of here in an hour..." I say.

"You're right."

He hands Daisy over, and my heart wobbles as she smiles up at me. "Hey, Sunshine," I say. "Aren't you all giggles this morning. Was your daddy telling you all his lame jokes again?"

"Hey, I can hear you," he gripes teasingly as he climbs the stairs. "Coffee is on," he calls out, as he disappears around the corner.

I put Daisy over my shoulder, and she makes noises as I head to the kitchen for a much needed cup of coffee. I walk around Jonah's big house. It's definitely going to have to be baby proofed before little Miss Sunshine starts crawling.

I continue to hold Daisy, not wanting to put her down as Jonah gets ready, and a short time later, we're buckling Daisy in and heading to the park.

My heart pinches a bit as I steal a glance at him. It's odd

how right this feels, the three off us heading out like a little family to meet my brother and father at the park.

Jonah pulls into an empty spot on the street, and I grab the stroller as he gets Daisy from the backseat. I shade my eyes, look around at all the kids and parents playing ball, Frisbee or flying a kite. Warmth bubbles up inside me, and this time I can't push it down.

In the distance, I spot a woman climbing from her car and staring at Jonah. I roll my eyes. Probably another one of his puck bunnies. How many of them will we run into today…and why does that rattle me so much?

An elderly woman walking her dog stops on the sidewalk and glances into the stroller. "She's so beautiful," she says, and Jonah smiles.

"Thanks."

Fine lines crinkle around the woman's eyes as her glance goes from the cooing baby to me. "She looks just like you," she says.

I stiffen and hold my hands up. "I'm not her mother," I say quickly.

She frowns and gives me a look of disbelief. "Really? Could have fooled me."

She walks away, and I spot Zander and my dad. Zander waves us over, and Jonah pushes the stroller beside me. Tears prick my eyes when I see my dad. He's aged so much over the last few months, the treatment taking its toll on him. His tired eyes light up when he sees us, and he tries to stand, but Zander stops him. I bend to give him a hug.

"Well, are you going to let me have a look at her or not," he says in a gruff voice, but underneath it all, he's a softie, like my brother…like me. Jonah might call me Ninja Chihuahua, and I am tough, I had to be. But like the rest of my family, I feel things deeply. "I'm not getting any younger, you know."

THE BODY CHECKER

Dad jerks his thumb toward Zander and me. "And these two don't seem to be in a hurry to give me grandchildren."

Jonah picks Daisy up and she fusses. "She's not your granddaughter by blood, but she's your granddaughter nonetheless," Jonah says, and I don't miss the way Dad's eyes cloud over. But he quickly blinks the emotions away and squints at Daisy.

"You're right, Zander. She does look like Winston Churchill." The two laugh, while Jonah and I find no humor in it.

"Great, a few minutes ago, a woman stopped to admire her and told me how much we look alike. Does that mean *I* look like Winston Churchill, too?" I ask, wanting to keep things light, as my father's sickness always overwhelms me.

"She kind of does look like you, Quinn," he says, and winks at me. "You sure you're not the mother? If you are, I expect that boy to put a ring on your finger," he says. His gaze goes from me to Zander. "Damned tired of waiting for the two of you to get married, too."

My heart misses a beat. "No, I'm not the mother."

I just want to be.

11

JONAH

It's so strange being here without Daisy. She's only been with us two weeks now, and I already feel the loss of her absence. But the only way I was going to get her room painted was by letting Quinn take her to work. They had an opening this week in the daycare, and at least I know she's in good hands. I chuckle to myself. It's kind of crazy how fast I've grown to care for the little girl.

My front door opens. "Jonah?" Zander calls out.

"Up here."

Zander takes my stairs two at a time, and cringes when he finds me in the baby's room. "Bubble-gum pink?"

"I like it," I say. "Now grab a brush and get rolling."

Zander shakes his head. "Did Quinn pick this color?"

"No, I did."

"Dude, come on. You're going to have to turn in your man card."

I laugh at him. "Wait and see the things you'll do for your own child, Zander."

"That's not going to be for a while."

"You do want kids though, right?

He gives an easy shrug. "When the time is right."

I dip my roller into the tray and load it. "Quinn says she never wants kids. How can a girl who works at a daycare, and is so good with Daisy, not want a family of her own?"

Zander grabs a roller, loads it, and starts on the wall opposite me. "I don't know. I guess that's something you'll have to ask her." A pause and then, "How are thing going between you two, anyway?"

My gut clenches. I hate lying to my best friend, but what the hell am I supposed to do? "We've been doing okay. She's a great help. I'm not looking forward to her leaving."

"Is that why none of the nannies are suitable? You want to keep Quinn here?"

I'm glad my back is to him, because the guy can read me like a book. One look at my face and he'd see right through me. That yes, none of the nannies are suitable, because none of the nannies are Quinn. I find fault with everyone we interview, and while Quinn does too, she keeps reminding me she's not going to be staying with us forever.

"She's just really good with kids. Daisy loves her."

"I think Quinn feels the same way about Daisy." I hear the worry in his voice.

"What?" I ask.

"I just don't want to see either of you hurt."

I go stiff and suck in a fast breath. "What do you mean?"

"What if Shari comes back, Jonah? What if she takes Daisy away?"

"I won't let that happen. She's my daughter too, and Shari just abandoned her." I turn and find Zander looking at me. "What she did was wrong. You of all people know that."

He nods. "I know, but...maybe you should talk to your dad, get some legal advice here."

I grip the back of my neck and rub as worry prowls through my body. "Where is all this coming from?" I ask, getting the sense that he knows something I don't.

"Yesterday, at the park. I was almost certain I saw Shari pull up in her car not too far behind you."

As soon as the words leave his mouth, my phone pings. I stare at it, my heart jumping into my throat.

"You better get that," Zander says.

I reach for my phone, and relax when I see it's a text from Quinn. But then a new kind of worry tears through me.

"What?" Zander asks when I tense.

"Daisy is running a fever. Quinn is bringing her home." I glance up from my phone. Here I thought I was getting the hang of things, but when push comes to shove, I have no idea how to help a sick child. Thank God for Quinn. "This is bad, isn't it?"

Zander steps up to me and puts his hand on my shoulder. "Kids get fevers all the time. It's probably just something she picked up at the park. Everyone was fussing all over her yesterday."

I nod, not convinced. "I should run to the drugstore to get some medication."

"Good idea. I'll stay here and paint and wait for Quinn."

I set my roller down, and I'm just about to shove my phone in my pocket when it pings again. I grab it, expecting it to be Quinn.

When I see who the text is from this time, the room goes fuzzy around the edges.

"Jonah?" Zander says. "What now? Is it...Daisy?"

I hold the phone out to show him the message from Shari, and he reads it out loud

Can I see you? Coffee at Feldman's tonight?

Concerned blue eyes meet mine, and he scrubs his hand over the back of his neck. "Shit, what are you going to do?"

"I don't know." I stare at the message. "Girls need their mothers, but after what she did…" I go quiet for a moment, mull this over then say, "Right now, I have to get Daisy her medicine. I'll deal with Shari later."

With my stomach twisted in knots, I head downstairs, grab my keys from the counter, and step outside. The sun is high in the sky, warming me instantly as I jump into my car and jack the air. I take off, head to the pharmacy to grab what I need, then return home to find Quinn's car in the driveway. Will Zander have filled her in? If so, how will she feel about Shari's text?

I hurry inside, and the three people I care about with everything in me are sitting in the living room. Quinn is fully focused on Daisy, and I get the sense Zander is waiting for me to tell her about Shari.

"How is she?" I ask and cross the room. I put my hand on her forehead, the way my mom used to do with me. She feels warm, but no warmer than usual. Man, I really suck at this. Her cheeks are flushed, and her eyes are a bit glossy.

"It's low-grade," Quinn explains, as I lift the paper bag and dump the medicine onto the coffee table. "Nothing to worry about, but we can't keep her at the daycare and risk other children catching it."

Zander laughs as the medicine spills from the bag, some landing on the floor. "Did you buy one of everything?"

"Yeah," I say and grip the back of my neck as I take in a fussing Daisy. "I wasn't sure what she needed."

"Children's acetaminophen will do," Quinn says, and I root through the boxes until I find what she needs. "Did you set her crib up in your bedroom?" she asks.

With the paint fumes, we planned for her to sleep with us anyway. Now I'm glad I moved her crib. I want her near me, to be able to keep a watchful eye on her. "Yeah. I didn't finish the painting, though."

"That's okay. I'm going to give her some medicine and put her to bed."

"Do you have to go back to work?" I ask, panic lacing my voice as I drop onto the sofa.

"No, I called in a sub. I figured you'd want me here to help Daisy." As if sensing her brother's gaze latched on her, her glance darts to Zander, and I see the way he's watching the two of us.

"Thanks," I say, and this time my phone rings. All eyes shoot to me. I grab my phone, check caller ID. "My parents," I say, and swipe my finger across the screen as Quinn heads to the stairs.

"Mom, hey, how's it going?"

"We're on our way to your place right now."

I briefly close my eyes. "Everything is under control," I say. "You didn't need to cut your vacation short."

"We wanted to. We've had time to think this over, and you're obviously going to need my help, and we want to see our grandchild, Jonah."

I nod, even though they can't see me. "I can understand that, but Quinn is just putting her to bed. She has a low-grade fever." I exhale softly. "I don't know what I would have done without Quinn." My eyes lift, and I note again the way Zander is staring at me.

"Did you give her children's acetaminophen?" she asks quickly.

I hear Dad in the background asking questions, then a car horn blares.

"I did. Quinn says it's nothing to worry about."

"Okay, good. We're almost there. See you shortly"

Zander stands after I end the call. "On that note, I'm out of here."

"What? You don't want to stay for the inquisition?" Not that I can blame him. I don't either.

"I'd do just about anything for you, pal. But you're on your own with this one." He puts his hand on my shoulder. "If you want to talk about Shari later, give me a call."

I grip my hair and tug. "Shit, yeah. I don't know what to do."

Zander leaves, and I walk him to the door. I step outside, sit on the front steps, and consider my next move with Shari. Is she calling because she wants Daisy back, or maybe she wants to work out some kind of arrangement? I can't say no. She's the child's mother, and I doubt the law would grant me full custody. They probably wouldn't like the idea of me being on the road and Daisy left with a nanny. If she was left with Quinn, however—

Wait, what the hell am I saying? I can't keep Quinn here with me forever. She has her own life, and she made it perfectly clear she wasn't interested in having a family. Zander said she was falling for Daisy. But that doesn't mean she wants to be her sole caregiver—her mother.

Unless she was falling for me too...

Damn. Damn. Damn.

I need to stop thinking like that. We're having sex, and she's not looking for more.

Am I?

Before I can answer that question, Mom and Dad pull into the driveway, and I stand. Mom jumps from the passenger seat and hurries to me. She cups my cheeks, looks me over.

"Have you been getting any sleep?"

"Yes," I say, even though I've been getting very little. "I'm fine, Mom." Dad steps up to me and we shake hands. "You didn't have to rush home."

"We wanted to, son. We want to meet your daughter," he says, but I can read between the lines. There's a full-on interrogation about to happen.

"Come on in, then."

They follow me inside and the air conditioning is a nice break from the heat. "Quinn put her to bed, so we need to keep our voices down." I lead them upstairs, and my pulse jumps when Quinn's soft voice reaches my ears. She's humming a lullaby to Daisy.

"Hey," I say quietly, and when she spins to see me, a soft smile on her mouth, I know I'm in fucking trouble. She glances past my shoulders.

"Oh, I didn't—"

"Mom and Dad came home early. They wanted to meet Daisy."

"Let me get out of your way."

I step up to her, and brush my knuckles over hers. "No, stay," I say, wanting her with me when my folks meet Daisy.

"Quinn," my mother says and gives her a hug. "It's so good to see you, and thank you for helping Jonah out. He told me he'd be lost without you."

Her eyes meet mine, and she smiles. "We're like family," she says, and this time I note that she's no longer calling me her brother. Good thing, because that's just wrong. But we *are* like family. At least for these last couple weeks we've been playing house. My dad greets Quinn, and then everyone turns their attention to a sleeping Daisy.

"Jonah, she's beautiful," Mom says.

I smile at that. Proud of my little girl.

"He's so good with her, Alice." Quinn puts her hand on my arm, and her heat sinks into my skin, curls around my heart. "You would be so proud of the way he's stepped up. I know I am."

My chest swells, and Mom gives me a little hug, but her eyes are on the way Quinn just touched me. "We raised him right," she says, a new light in her eyes as she focuses back in on me. She studies me for a minute, and I catch a spark of something in her eyes before she looks away. Damn, does she know what Quinn and I've really been doing?

"That you did," Quinn says. "You should be proud."

Mom leans into the crib. "I can't wait to hold her."

"She'll likely sleep for a few hours," Quinn says, and tucks a light blanket around the baby. "The medicine knocked her out."

"Let's let her sleep." Mom smiles. "There will be plenty of time for hugs later," she says and ushers us out of the room, but Quinn stays behind.

"I haven't finished my lullaby," she says, and I get the sense that she wants to stay upstairs to watch over Daisy.

"We're all so very lucky to have you," Mom says before we head downstairs.

"Drink?" I ask, and they both shake their heads no as they sit, clearly wanting to get to the heart of matters.

"You seem to have everything under control, Jonah," my mother says. "Quinn is quite something. She really cares about that child. Very maternal, a nurturer by nature."

Before I can answer, Dad pipes in. "What will you do when practice starts up in a couple of weeks? When you have to go back on the road again?" He leans forward and steeples his fingers like he always does when he's serious. "You've worked too long and hard for your career, Jonah. It's all you ever wanted." He pauses, then adds, "What can your mother and I do to help you manage all this?"

"It's okay, Dad. I appreciate the offer, but Quinn and I have been searching for a nanny."

"How is that going?" Mom asks.

"Slow. We've interviewed a few people, but I want to make sure I pick the right one. I don't want to leave my child with just anyone."

Mom nods. "Totally understandable, which leads me to my next question. Where is her mother?"

"She dropped her off one morning and vanished," I say. "I hadn't heard from her until today."

"She contacted you?" Dad asks.

She wants to meet me for coffee tonight." The stairs creak and I glance up to see Quinn, and she grimaces.

"Oh, sorry. I didn't mean to intrude," she says. "I...ah...just want to grab that ear thermometer." She hurries into the room and avoids looking at me as she grabs the new thermometer off the coffee table. A second later, she's back upstairs, and I have two sets of concerned eyes staring at me.

"Do you think she's going to try to take Daisy away?" Mom asks in a panic. She turns to Dad. "Your father will fight it in court, won't you, Donald?"

He holds his hands up. "Before we get ahead of ourselves, you're going to need to meet with her and talk to her. For all we know, maybe she wants you both back."

I don't bother telling him that what I had with Shari was only a fling. There was never anything meaningful or deeper. I've never wanted that with anyone...until now.

Shit.

"I mean, a child does need a mother and a father, right?" Dad says.

"Yeah," I agree.

"Maybe you should be thinking of doing the right thing." I brace myself for what's coming next. "Hockey is the most important thing in the world to you, so maybe you should get married, then your daughter will be cared for by her rightful mother, freeing you of worry when you go back on the road."

Rightful mother?

How does she have any rights when she up and abandoned her daughter—leaving her with a guy like me—without so much as leaving me a car seat, or a contact number if anything goes wrong? Quinn stepped up to the bat without question. Quinn should be Daisy's mother, goddammit. Too bad a family is the last thing in the world she wants.

12

QUINN

With Jonah out meeting Shari for coffee, and Daisy asleep in the master suite, I finish the painting in her room, needing something to occupy my hands and my thoughts. Nervous energy wells up inside me and I can't stop my mind from racing, from playing out every possible scenario.

Ever since I overheard Jonah's parents telling him he should do the right thing, I've been a mess.

Do I think he should marry the mother of his child? Hell no. Why should they set themselves up for that kind of disaster, and in the end, it's only going to hurt Daisy. Jonah will come to resent Shari, the same way my mom came to resent Dad after they had kids. Eventually she left to pursue dreams a family kept her from, and if hockey is Jonah's true love, and he's not ready for this, he just might end up leaving everyone behind, too.

I finish the last touches on the wall and stand back to admire the color. It's bright, but I'm sure Daisy will love it. I wipe my hand across my forehead and drop the brush into the tray just as the downstairs door opens. My heart leaps into my throat. I'm anxious to hear how tonight went, but I'm also terrified. What if he does follow his parents' advice? What if he comes up here and asks me to pack my things?

Why do I have to keep reminding myself we're just having sex while playing house?

His footsteps are slow, and I sense his trepidation, like he's not in a hurry to share the news with me. I suck in a breath and let it out slowly to prepare myself. I step into the hall to meet him and he's rubbing the back of his neck as he comes close. Never a good sign.

"Hey," I say, and he glances up. He smiles when he sees me, and my stomach flips. "You okay?" I ask, even though it's clear he's not.

He nods. "How is Daisy?" He looks at his bedroom door.

"Sleeping quietly. She had something to eat and her fever is coming down. I think she was just teething." He nods, walks past me, and steps into the bedroom for a second to check on her, something any good father would do. My heart swells. He may not have been a natural with her, but the bond is growing and even without conscious thought, he's putting her well-being first.

When he comes back out, his gaze rakes the length of me. "You've been painting?"

"I finished her room off. Come see. It looks great."

We both step into the room and he looks around, but it's easy to tell he's preoccupied. I want to ask what Shari wanted, but I bite my tongue. He turns back to me and the corners of his mouth curve. "You have paint on your face," he says quietly, and wipes at my forehead.

"I know. I'm a mess," I say. It's true, I *am* a mess. In more ways than one.

He shoves his hands into his pockets, and his jeans ride low on his hips. "I was thinking about jumping into the pool. Do a few laps, cool down."

I nod. "Okay."

He arches a brow. "Join me?"

"I don't have a suit."

"You don't need one. Back yard is private." He glances over my shoulder and his hand captures mine. He's in such a weird mood, I don't know what to make of it. "We'll take the baby monitor out with us, in case Daisy wakes."

He guides me into the hallway and keeps his hand in mine as we make our way down the stairs. I grab the baby monitor, and we step out into the warm night. Jonah makes quick work of his clothes, and I admire his body, more tense than usual as he dives into the deep end and does a few fast laps. I undress, fold my clothes and place them on a chair, and make my way to the shallow end. I dip my toe in and shiver.

Jonah surfaces at the other end. "It's cold," I say, and he laughs.

"Not once you're in." I tentatively take the first step. "You have to the count of three, then I'm coming to get you."

"You wouldn't," I yell, but I'm happy to see he's his old playful self.

"Try me."

Dammit, I know him well enough to know he'll follow through. I hurry to the next step, and goose bumps break out on my skin.

"Time's up." Jonah dives under the water, and I track him as I take the third step. He comes up in front of me and I squeal. His arms go around me, and while he's making me wet and cold, I don't want to push him away.

His lips find mine, and he falls backward, kissing me as we both go under. I wrap my arms around him and hold on. We finally surface and both gasp for air.

"You okay?" I ask, and he shakes his head no.

Worry takes up residency in my gut as he dives back under and does a few more laps. I leave him be. He obviously needs space to think right now. He eventually comes up in front of me again, and wipes the water from his eyes.

"She wants us to be a family," he says.

My heart falls into my stomach, and I take his hand and guide him to the steps.

"What did you tell her?"

"I don't know what to tell her, Quinn. I get that Daisy needs her mother, but I don't love her." His dark eyes meet mine, glisten in the pool lights. He opens his mouth like he wants to say something, then closes it again.

"I overheard what your mother and father said to you today. I didn't mean to, but I was headed down the stairs and couldn't help but hear."

His hand goes to my thigh and he splays his fingers. "They want me to do the right thing."

I take his hand in mine, give it a small squeeze. "But is being with Shari the right thing?"

"They seem to think so."

"What do you think?"

"I don't know."

"If you find a good nanny, one who can care for Daisy, you guys could co-parent. Share custody."

He stiffens and takes his hand from mine.

What the hell? Was it something I said?

"She said it's either the two of them, or neither of them."

Enraged, I blurt out, "She can't do that. You're Daisy's father, you have every right to see your child. I'm sure your father will take this to court."

"I'm sure he'll tell me I need to do the right thing. He's old school, Quinn. They had me late in life and look at things differently than we do."

I shake my head, astounded at this turn of events. "If it's the two of them or neither, why did she just drop Daisy off with you?"

A noise crawls out of his throat. "She wanted us to bond."

I briefly close my eyes and try to look at this situation from all angles. One thought jumps out at me. "Why now, Jonah? Why four months later?"

"Think about it," he says, and frowns.

Something niggles at the back of my mind, and I reach for it. "Wait, do you think this is about money? You just had a successful season, and renewed your contract for some serious coin."

He makes a noise, half laugh, half snort. "That's right. It's always about the money, Quinn. Do you think any of these women are with us for anything other than our fame and fortune? No one sees us for who we are. They never want to know the person beneath the jersey. It's just the way it is."

I put my hand on his back and lean into him. "I had no idea, Jonah." I mull that over for a minute. "Is that why you're so anti-marriage?"

He turns to me, his eyes dark and tortured. A long pause as his eyes search my face, then he says, "I wouldn't say I was anti-marriage, it was just something I never thought about, something that was a long way off. I guess that could change, it I was with the right woman."

Oh, God, Quinn. Tell him how you feel.

Take a chance? But what if I make a fool of myself? What if I'm imagining there could be more between us? Imagining I'm the right woman? I open my mouth, but no words come. Where the hell is Ninja Chihuahua when I really need her?

"It's not my business, Jonah, I get that, but if you marry her, I think you're going to grow to regret it." I fold my arms around my body and hug myself. "I know this from experience," I say softly

His eyes narrow, and he looks at me, searches my face for answers. "What do you mean?"

I exhale a long breath. "Mom never wanted a family. It

was Dad. He wanted kids. Mom wanted a career. She ended up having two kids, but in the end, even though she loved us, her first love *wasn't* us, so she left." Tears prick my eyes and I pinch them tight. "Growing up without a mother was hard. I'm not going to lie. Dad sort of shrank into himself. I don't know what I would have done it I didn't have Zander."

He puts his arm around me, drags me to his body. Water ripples around us, and I grow chilly, not just from the air but from my memories.

"I'm sorry, Quinn."

"I'm just worried about Daisy," I say. "Your first love is hockey, Jonah. I know you care for that little girl, but what happens in the end? Will you grow to resent Shari and Daisy, and leave?"

"I'm not your mother," he says, his voice taking on a hard edge.

"I never said you were, but the circumstances...I don't want to see Daisy..." I let my words fall off as a fine shiver goes through me.

"Is that why you don't want a family or kids?" he asks, as things grow personal between us.

I take a long moment, then say, "My parents failed so badly at marriage, and it wasn't easy being abandoned. I just... don't want to set myself up for that."

Jonah opens his mouth like he wants to say something, closes it again, and stands. "You're cold. Let's get inside."

He grabs our towels, and wraps one around me and the other around himself. Then he gathers our clothes, as well as the baby monitor, and we both go inside. Where we go from here, I'm not certain. Will he even want me in his house tonight if he's contemplating marriage to another woman? Do I even *want* to be in his house if he's contemplating marriage to another woman?

"Glass of wine?" he asks, his voice less harsh as I take in his bare upper body.

I nod, and he grabs a chilled bottle of white from the fridge and two glasses. He pours and we both take a much needed sip. Little cries come from the baby monitor, and we set our glasses down.

"Go relax and have your wine, Quinn. I'll check on Daisy, then I'll join you." He lets his towel fall and climbs back into his clothes. I don't bother dressing. Instead, I make my way into the living room and flick on the television, giving Jonah alone time with his daughter. It seems to be what he needs right now.

I hear Jonah's voice through the baby monitor as he changes Daisy's diaper and cuddles her. I sip my wine and flick through the stations, my heart so invested in this family, I'm sure to fall to pieces once I have to leave them. I settle on a rerun and things go quiet upstairs. I glance at the clock. It's not late, but I have a feeling Jonah fell asleep rocking his little girl.

Deciding I might as well get a good night's sleep too, I turn the television off and stand. I stretch out my limbs, but when a hard knock sounds on the door, I nearly jump out of my skin.

I hurry across the room and look through the peephole. There is a girl on the stoop, but I don't recognize her. She sways a little, and runs her hands over her long dark hair, like she's trying to make herself presentable. I wait, debate on what to do, but then she knocks again. Harder this time.

"Jonah, open up," she says, and then hiccups.

OMG, is she drunk?

I push back from the door and turn when I hear footsteps coming my way. "Jonah," I say, as he rubs his eyes.

"What's going on?" he asks.

"There's a girl on the steps. I think she's drunk."

"Shit." He looks through the peephole, then swings the door open wide. The girl gives him a seductive smile—but then her eyes go wide when they see me...in nothing but my towel.

"What the hell are you doing here?" she spits out, and leans her hand on the side of the house to keep her balance.

"I...uh..." I say and step back.

"What do you want, Shari?"

Holy hell, this is Shari.

"I want my daughter," she says, and tries to push past Jonah, but he won't allow it. He grips her shoulders and holds her in place.

"Let go of me! I'm getting my daughter and taking her home."

"You're not going anywhere with her."

Her eyes are venomous when they connect with mine. "I'll phone the police."

"Go ahead. You've been drinking, and now you're behind the wheel. If you want to end up in the drunk tank tonight, make the call. Let's see how fast you get your daughter back after that."

She changes tactics, and sags against Jonah, running her fingers along his chest. "What we talked about earlier, Jonah. You said you were going to think about it. You can't blame me for being mad when I find you here with another girl."

"Quinn is Zander's sister. She's been helping me with Daisy until I could find a nanny. You should be thanking her."

Quinn is Zander's sister.

Those words shouldn't sting quite as much as they do. We did, after all, agree to keep what's going on behind closed doors a secret. And the truth is, I *am* Zander's sister, and maybe I should remember that's all I am to Jonah.

"Oh, I didn't realize." Instead of thanking me, she says, "I can't drive home. Do you think I could spend the night here?"

"Jonah, I should go," I say quickly, and his gaze flashes to mine, worry blazing in his eyes.

"No, I'm taking Shari home." His eyes search mine, like he's trying to see if I'm okay. "Would you mind watching Daisy? She can't drive like this. It's lucky she made it here without killing someone."

"No problem," I say, and back up until I'm on the first step.

Jonah leans Shari against a wall and heads to the kitchen to grabs his keys, leaving me alone in the front entrance with Shari.

"Why are you in a towel?" she asks. She points a finger at me. "You trying to take my man away from me?"

"I was swimming," I say, and tighten the towel around my body.

She steps toward me, wobbles a little. "You keep your hands to yourself. He's *mine*. I didn't go through all the trouble of having a kid for nothing."

My heart crashes against my chest and my brain spins in my head. She trapped Jonah! Oh, my God, she trapped Jonah by having a kid.

Jonah stalks back into the room, the muscles along his jaw rippling as he clenches his teeth together. His eyes meet mine and soften. "Thanks," he says, and I make a move to reach for him, tell him what's going on, stop this from happening. But as I do, Shari falls into him, wrapping her arms around his body in a show of possession.

"Bye, Queenie," she says, and I'm about to tell her off, but Jonah speaks first. Probably a good thing. I don't want to get in the middle of a fight or do anything that could mess up the relationship between him and his daughter.

"Here name is Quinn," Jonah says, his voice rough, angry.

"Isn't that a guy's name?" She looks me over again, and I

resist the urge to throat punch her. "Then again, I guess she could pass as one," she says, and laughs.

Jonah goes ramrod straight, holds her by the shoulders and pulls her off his body. "Being drunk is no excuse for being rude. You have no idea what she's been doing for our daughter."

"What's she been doing for *you*, Jonah?" she flings back at him

"That's none of your business."

She reaches out, cups his cock, and says, "As long as she knows this is mine."

Jonah removes her hand, tosses me an apologetic look, and practically drags her out the door.

"You think about what I said, Queenie. Or I'll lawyer up, and Jonah will never get to see his daughter again!"

I stand there, legs too numb to move, as Jonah locks the door behind himself. It's only when I hear her car start up that I'm able to breathe again.

I lower myself onto the step and think about calling my best friend. But Jonah's business is his, and it wouldn't be right of me to tell secrets. I pick myself up and fight back the tears. I turn, deciding to go to bed, when my cell rings.

I rush to it, and my heart races when I see it's from Zander.

"Hey," I say.

"You okay?" he asks, and I hear the concern in his voice.

"Not really."

"Jonan called me. I'm going to pick him up at Shari's and bring him home. He asked me to check in on you. He said Shari was pretty nasty. I know you can handle yourself but still."

Tears threaten, and I wipe them away. Not because of anything Shari said, but because of Daisy, Jonah. They're both in a terrible position. "I'm okay."

"Hey, it's me," he says, his voice softening. "I know you're not."

"Zander, she basically said she trapped him."

He blows out a breath, then says, "I figured it was something like that. Jonah's always careful."

"He doesn't deserve any of this," I say, my voice a little choked. "He's one of the good guys, Zander."

He gives a small laugh, because he probably never thought he'd hear those words from me. "Yeah, I know. I've always known."

"What is she after?"

"Fame and fortune," he says.

This time the tears do fall. My emotions are on a goddamn roller coaster ride. "I feel so sorry for Daisy, she's the one who's going to get hurt in all this."

"So are you and Jonah. I know how much you've fallen for that little girl. Hang on, I'm just getting into the car. Going to put you on speaker."

I wipe my eyes, my heart going out to the innocent child asleep upstairs. To the man who has no idea which way to turn.

"Okay, you there?"

"I'm here," I say.

"Jonah's dad is a lawyer. He'll get this figured out."

"Maybe so, but there will be damage."

"You sound tired. Why don't you get to sleep. I'll have Jonah back to you soon."

The phone tightens in my hands. God, the way he just said that makes it sound like Jonah is mine. He's not.

Oh, but you want him to be.

"Okay, thanks, Zander. Love you."

"Love you, too."

With that, I hang up, and my tears fall as I walk upstairs

and find Daisy sleeping soundly. I touch her hair, brush my hand lightly over it.

"I have no idea what's going to happy, little one, but I promise you, I'll do anything to help protect you. Anything at all."

She makes a small sound, and I could have sworn she understood what I was saying and was thanking me for it.

13
JONAH

"Thanks for the lift," I say to Zander as I climb from his car. The cooler night air falls around me and I stretch out, my mind running a million miles an hour after coffee with Shari. Although coffee didn't happen. She texted me, said to meet her at her favorite club, and eventually conversation turned into her hands all over me.

"Talk to your dad. See what he has to say," Zander says before I shut the door.

"I will." I close the door quietly, not wanting to wake anyone in the neighborhood, and stand back to glance at my house.

The lights are off, all except the front porch. A warm glow falls over the steps and walkway, guiding me to my front door, and that brings a smile to my face. Quinn left the light on for me. It shouldn't surprise me. She's the most giving, caring woman I know, and I should have kicked Shari for being so fucking rude to her. I push down the anger and pull my keys from my pocket. Zander takes off as I make my way inside.

The house is quiet. Just like old times. I laugh at that.

Here I used to cherish my bachelorhood, and never gave much thought to settling down. But I suddenly don't like the stillness of the house. I make my way upstairs, walking quietly so I don't wake my girls. My bedroom door is open slightly, and I step inside.

I check on Daisy first, press my hand to her forehead. She's much cooler than she was earlier. Maybe Quinn was right and she's teething.

I glance at my bed, and sensations well up inside me, curl around my heart, when I find Quinn there, fast asleep. If I had to put a name to what I'm feeling, I'd have to call it want, need…love.

Love?

Is it possible that I'm falling in love with my best friend's kid sister? Not a smart move on my part, that's for fucking sure.

I make quick work of my clothes and slide into the bed. Quinn stirs beside me, and I shimmy closer until I'm spooning her. Her body is warm from sleep, and her fresh scent swirls around me. I put one hand on her hip and hold her to me.

As I lay there, my mind and body tired after dealing with Shari, my thoughts drift. Zander is right. I do need to call my father. I'm sure, after the stunt Shari just pulled, and her threatening to lawyer up to keep Daisy away from me if I don't follow her demands, he'll change his tune on what's right and what isn't.

My mind races back to the gut-wrenching story Quinn told me about her mother. It must have been hard for her to open up to me like that. But I get she was trying to make a point, save Daisy from a hard future. The thing is, I'm not Quinn's mother, but how can I take care of a child if I'm on the road all the time? Everyone keeps telling me hockey is the most important thing in the world to me.

Would I grow to regret the responsibility? Am I that fucking shallow?

My thoughts fall off and the next thing I know, I'm in bed alone. I sit up, rub the blur from my eyes and check Daisy's crib. She's not in it. I kick off the covers and tug on a pair of jeans. From downstairs, I hear a kid's movie with lots of music playing in the background. After a quick trip to the bathroom, I make my way down, find Daisy in Quinn's arms as they dance around the living room.

Right then and there, my heart swells in my chest, and it's almost difficult to breathe. I grab the banister, squeeze my hand around it. Fuck. Shit. And Damn.

This...*this* is the family I want.

Quinn squeals and lets out an embarrassed laugh when she turns and finds me standing there.

"Good morning," I say.

"I really am getting you a bell." Pink spreads across her cheeks as Daisy giggles up at her. "Did we wake you?"

I shake my head. "Did Daisy just laugh."

A smile lights up Quinn's face. "She did. They usually start laughing around four months. I thought she would have done it long before now, actually."

"Shit."

"What?"

"I don't even know when her birthday is. She could be five months now and I wouldn't even know it."

"We should get her in for a checkup. We need to find out who her doctor is, and see if she's all up to date with her immunizations."

I nod. Another conversation with Shari that I'm not looking forward too. "Don't you have to be at work?"

"I took the next couple of days off. I thought you might need me here if Shari comes around like that again."

"I need to call my dad."

"Good idea."

I grab my phone from my back pocket and pull up Dad's contact. I'm guessing he'd be at his office already so I call that number. It rings twice, and his receptionist picks up. I tell her who I am, and she transfers me through right away.

Quinn turns the television down and takes Daisy into the kitchen to give me privacy. Dad answers, and I explain everything to him.

He goes quiet for a long time.

"You still there?" I finally ask.

"It's not a good situation for you, son, especially with you being on the road, and the courts do favor the mother."

I rest my elbows on my knees and exhale. "What can I do? I can't let her get full custody."

"There is one thing that could help you."

"What? Anything?"

"If you can prove you're a family man and have Daisy's best interests at heart."

"How am I supposed to do that?"

"By getting married?"

I briefly pinch my eyes shut, trying to decipher what he's saying. "I told you, I can't marry her. I don't love her, and after the stunt she just pulled, I'm not even sure I want her around my daughter."

Just then, Quinn steps into the room, and her eyes are wide. I shake my head at her, at a loss.

"Son, I'm not suggesting you marry her. I was suggesting you marry someone else."

"Marry someone else?" I ask. "Like who?" Quinn walks across the room, and Daisy grabs her hair and giggles. Quinn winces and very carefully removes Daisy's hand from her hair as they head upstairs.

"What about Quinn?"

Before I can stop myself, I blurt out, "You think I should marry Quinn?"

Quinn stops halfway up the stairs and slowly turns around. As if her legs are about to give out on her, she sinks down, sits on the step. Our eyes meet, and lock.

"It's like this. It doesn't have to be a real marriage, just one for show. You two go way back. She's a nice girl, works at a daycare. How much better could it be?"

"I can't ask Quinn to do something like that. She has a life of her own. She's done enough for us as it is."

"Then make her an offer she can't refuse. If you can prove to the courts you're a stable family man, with someone to care for Daisy when you're on the road, they're more likely to rule in your favor. You might not get full custody, but you should get shared."

I shake my head, hardly able to believe what my Dad is suggesting. It might look good to the courts, but no way in hell would a girl, not interested in a family of her own, agree to marry a man with a child.

"Just think about it, son. You could have a quick ceremony at city hall, and once things are settled, you could get an annulment."

"Do you think that's the right thing for Daisy, though?" I ask. "What about when I'm on the road, who's going to take care of her?"

"Your mother and I have discussed that, and she will."

My head rears back, surprised. "Daisy's not Mom's responsibility, she's mine."

"Then she'll care for her until you find yourself a real wife, someone who will love and care for Daisy as much as you."

"I have to go," I say, and slide my finger across the screen to end the call.

I look up again, and my eyes land on Quinn. As I take her in, see the way she cares for Daisy, I realize I've already found that woman. If only she felt the same way about me. Her brother would rip off my left nut, but I'm pretty sure I can live without one.

I open my mouth to speak, but she holds her hand up to cut me off. Not that I blame her. I think the idea of a fake marriage is insane, too. Especially when it's a real one I want.

"I'll do it," she says.

14

QUINN

What the hell am I doing?

Standing before a Justice of the Peace in city hall, I hold the flowers in my hand and glance at the handsome man beside me. Goddammit, he looks so incredible in his suit, my entire body vibrates with need.

Zander, his best man, stands beside him, and my best friend Tina is to my left. I feel crappy for keeping her out of the loop for so long, but I'd been so caught up in Jonah and Daisy, I had very little time for anything else. I plan to make that up to her though, once things settle down and our lives are in order.

From behind us, Daisy coos and both Jonah and I turn at the same time, so attuned to all her little sounds. She's smiling and pulling on his mother's hair, but she doesn't seem to mind. She's going to make a wonderful grandmother, and for that I'm grateful.

Dad is sitting in his wheelchair, and guilt niggles at me. He's the only one not privy to the ruse, and I'd prefer to keep it that way. He'd love to see his daughter married before his cancer took him, and I'm happy I can do this for him. He coughs, and I turn back to the man about to marry us.

I'm marrying Jonah Long.

We exchange vows, and when Jonah puts his grandmother's ring on my finger, I'm still in awe that his mother insisted. Why would she want me to wear it? Shouldn't it be saved for someone special, someone Jonah loves? Then again, I guess when this ruse is over, she'll be getting it back.

After the exchange of rings, we're told to kiss, and Jonah takes me into his arms. He brushes his knuckle along my cheek, a caress so soft and tender, I have to remind myself this marriage isn't real. His smile is slow as he leans into me, and when his lips touch mine, my heart pounds in my chest. His lips linger, and his hand tighten around my back to pull me close.

Zander clears his throat, and Jonah breaks the kiss.

I catch Zander's eye—and he grins at me.

My pulse jumps. Why do I get the feeling that he knows what we're doing behind closed doors? But if he does, why isn't he saying something?

The ceremony is over quickly, and once all the proper papers are signed, we leave city hall. Jonah takes Daisy from his mother, and I glance around, half-expecting Shari to pounce. But she's nowhere to be found. In fact, for the last couple of weeks, since Jonah took her home drunk that night, she's been gone. Rumor had it she was on a drinking binge, off partying with friends. At least Zander was able to get the information on Daisy's doctor, and after this ceremony, that's where we'll be taking her.

No reception.

No honeymoon.

No nothing.

It's not a real marriage.

Outside, the sunshine beats down on us as everyone

makes their ways to their cars. I give Dad a kiss before Zander helps him into the passenger seat of Zander's car. I look for Jonah, find him talking to his parents. Tina steps up to me, but she has a worried look on her face.

"You okay?"

"I'm good."

She nudges me. "Hey, it's your wedding day, you should be smiling."

I force a smile. "I am. See?"

"I was afraid of this."

I shade the sun from my eyes. "Afraid of what?"

"You like him. You really like him."

I'm about to protest, but this is my best friend and she can see right through me. "Yeah, I know."

"And you love that little girl."

Jonah bounces Daisy in his arms and she laughs out loud. An invisible band squeezes my heart. "I do. But it's not like that for him, Tina. I'm just doing him a favor. He wants me with him for Daisy."

Oh, how I wish he wanted me for him, too.

"Maybe you're wrong. Did you ever think of that?"

My gaze flies to hers. "What makes you say that?"

Her eyes go wide. "Ah, did you not see the way he kissed you?"

I shrug, too afraid to believe we could have more. Too afraid of getting hurt. What if we did give this family thing a go, and he decided hockey was more important? My God, why did I ever agree to this?

Because I promised Daisy I'd do whatever I had to in order to protect her.

But when I really thing about it, my actions won't be any different than my own mother's. Daisy will grow accustomed to me and in the end, when Jonah secures custody, I'll be out of the picture, abandoning her, the way my mother abandoned me.

"...Quinn."

"What?"

Jonah laughs. "You were a million miles away. What were you thinking about?"

"Daisy," I say quickly, honestly.

Tina puts her hand on my arm. "I'll leave you two newlyweds alone now. Shoot me a text and let me know how Daisy makes out with the doctor." She gives me a hug and heads to her car.

Jonah smiles at me and Daisy stretches her arms out. I take her from him, and she blows wet bubbles on my face. We both laugh, but then the smile falls from Jonah's face. He puts his hand on my hip, looks me over, takes in the white dress I bought off the rack at a local dress shop.

"You look beautiful," he says.

"This old thing?" I tease, but truthfully I agonized over the right dress to wear, wanting to look nice for Jonah. Here I never thought I'd get married, let alone wear a wedding dress and step into a ready-made family.

"Thank you, Quinn. For everything."

"Anything for Daisy," I say.

Anything for you.

But I keep that to myself.

He nods, and his hand drops from my side. "I guess we should get home and get changed before her appointment."

I follow him to his car and slide into the front seat as he buckles Daisy in. She's happy and grabbing at her toys, and that warms my heart. Jonah settles himself into the driver's seat and pulls into traffic. I still find it amusing how slow he drives with Daisy in the car. We get home and I go upstairs to change out of my 'wedding dress' as he prepares her bottle. I pull on a light sundress, and take the baby from Jonah to give him time to change. He comes down looking like sin in a pair of cargo shorts and a T-shirt that showcases his beautiful muscles.

"I'll get the bag ready," he says, and I follow him as I burb the baby.

"Why are you putting so much into her diaper bag?"

"I like to be prepared?"

"For what, a zombie apocalypse?"

He laughs. "Who knows how long it will take at the doctor's office?"

I roll my eyes at him. "I'm guessing we won't be there overnight, Jonah." Daisy gives me a big burp, and I take her upstairs to put her in something more comfortable than the frilly dress I had a great time picking out for her.

Once we're all ready, we head outside, and I scan the street, always expecting Shari to pounce and try to get her daughter back. Once we're settled into the car, Jonah drives like he's at a snail convention as we head downtown. Good thing we left a lot of time.

We pull into the parking lot, and he gets his little girl from the back. He's so much more at ease holding her now. I reach into the backseat and grab her diaper bag, which weighs a ton. The elevator takes us to the tenth floor, and I read the list of names on panels to figure out where we're headed.

Once inside the office, I register Daisy and Jonah sits. I lower myself into the chair next to him and smile at the pregnant woman trying to get a glimpse of Daisy.

"How old is she?" she asks.

"Close to five months," Jonah says, even though we're not quite sure about that.

"She looks like you," the woman says, and when I glance up, it's me she's looking at, not Jonah.

"I've been told," I say.

The receptionist calls us in, and I grab the bag and follow Jonah. We step into the examination room, and the doctor smiles—but it falls off as she checks her chart. "Is this appointment for Daisy?"

"I'm her father," Jonah says. "I've been taking care of her."

"Oh." The doctor's gaze goes from Jonah, to me, back to Jonah.

"This is Quinn, she's been helping me out," he explains.

"Is everything okay with Daisy?" The doctor leans forward to check on the baby.

"I haven't had much contact with her mother, so we just want to make sure everything is up to date."

She opens the file, and frowns. "Jonah, you're not listed as the father. No one is." She hesitates. Papers flip as she goes through her file again. She bites on her bottom lip. "It looks here like she's just about ready for her four-month shot."

Jonah's gaze shoots to me.

"How old is she?" I ask.

"Uh..." the doctor says. "You don't know?"

"Her mother dropped her at my door weeks ago, telling me that I was her father and she's four months old. I figured she was closer to five months now," Jonah says.

"Well, let's see...she's just about four months old," she says. "But I really shouldn't be saying more, since you're not listed as the father."

Jonah frowns, and he looks down, like he's trying to figure something out. "Was she late being born?"

"Ah, I think you should talk to the mother," the doctor suggests.

Jonah and I nod, wanting answers, but not pushing because she's willing to give her a checkup and her four-month shot. He hands Daisy over, and I put my hand on his tense shoulder. I'm sure his thoughts are running along the same line as mine, and he's just as enraged that Shari neglected to tell him she needed her needles. He closes his hand over mine and squeezes. Thank God Daisy is with her father and not her mother. Who knows if she'd get the care she needs.

The doctor takes her weight and measures her, giving her a thorough check over, and then Jonah holds her as she prepares the needle. Daisy is happy on his lap, but his chest is rising and falling erratically, like this is killing him.

"Hi, Daisy," the doctor says, talking to her as she puts the needle in. Daisy bursts out crying, and Jonah swallows, hard.

"It's okay, little one," he whispers, and when the doctor is finished, I hug both Jonah and Daisy tight.

"Thanks," I say, and gather up her supplies. The doctor hands us a brochure, and I put it in my pocket. By the time we reach the car, Daisy has calmed down.

"Poor girl," I whisper, and I rub her back as Jonah unlocks the car.

Once Daisy is buckled in, Jonah slides into the driver's seat and exhales. I put my hand on his leg. "I think that might have been harder for Daddy."

He shakes his head and grunts. "I hope that's the last of her shots."

"Afraid not," I say as he starts the car.

"Why do you think Shari didn't tell me her real age?"

Worry goes through me, but I don't want to say too much. It's possible she could have been in the womb longer, late being born, but how long do they let babies go these days? But what if she hadn't been late in coming? What if...? My pulse thrums.

"Quinn...do you think..." His words fall off, like he can't bring himself to say them or believe them.

My mind races. Daisy has to be his child, right? Why would Shari just drop her off like that if she wasn't his? "She was probably late coming into this world," I say, knowing we're going to have to talk to Shari and get some answers.

He nods, and instead of going back to his place, he takes a turn and heads in the opposite direction. I frown and glance around. "Where are you going?"

His mood changes, and he gives me a mischievous grin. "You'll see."

15
JONAH

Quinn's face holds a measure of panic when she glances at me. "We should go straight home. Daisy needs rest after her shot."

"Where we're going, she's going to get plenty of rest."

"Where are we going?" she asks, a little more demanding.

I cast her a quick glance, and her arms are folded, her lips pinched tight. "Don't like surprises, Quinn?"

"You know I don't."

"You're right. I do. You certainly didn't like it when I surprised you and your friend with those concert tickets to your favorite band when you were sixteen."

Her face softens, and she turns from me. "That's different."

"A surprise is a surprise."

"The big surprise was that I had to go with you and Zander. What fun was that for a sixteen-year-old?"

"You think I was going to let two sixteen-year-olds go to a concert in the city by themselves?"

"I can take care of myself," she says, trying to look pissed off, but I see the way her lips are twitching.

"I know, and I can take care of you, too."

Her body relaxes. "Yeah, you sure can." A moment of silence, and then, "Did I ever thank you for those tickets, Jonah? I could be so bitchy back then."

"Back then?"

"Hey," she says and whacks me.

We finally pull up in front of my parents' house, and Quinn frowns. "Why are we here?"

Instead of answering, I exit the car and gather up Daisy. Mom and Dad come running from the house.

"There's my little girl," Mom says, and scoops Daisy from my hands. She gives me a kiss on the cheek as Quinn steps from the car.

"Jonah?" she asks. "What's going on?"

"What's going on, is Mom and Dad are going to watch Daisy. It is, after all, our wedding night."

She glances at the ring on her finger, then alarm moves across her face. "We can't leave Daisy. What if she cries or fusses? She just had her shot."

Mom laughs. "This isn't my first rodeo, child. Now go." She waves us away. "It's your wedding night."

Quinn shakes her head, and her short blonde hair wisps over her chin. "I...well...you'll call if she fusses?"

Mom nods as I grab the big diaper bag from the backseat and hand it to Dad. "Sure."

"Oh...okay, then," Quinn says, and steps up to Daisy to give her a kiss.

"You two kids go and have fun," Dad says.

We get back into the car, and Quinn's eyes are wide and wild when they turn my way. "Why didn't you tell me you were doing that?"

"I wanted it to be a surprise." I pull into traffic and take a left instead of a right.

"So that's what the diaper bag was all about. Wait, your house is back that way." She glares at me, that same deadly look she gave me the first day she showed up to help out with Daisy. "*Now* where are we going, Jonah?"

"Now *there's* the Ninja Chihuahua I know and love."

She punches me in the shoulder and it damn well hurts. "Ow," I say. "Who taught you to hit like that?"

"You, remember?"

I laugh. "I remember. A girl has to protect herself. I'll be teaching Daisy those same moves."

She laughs with me. "Good thing Daisy will have me, then."

"A really good thing," I say, and slide my hand across the seat to capture hers.

She looks away from me, stares out the window and takes in the city as I drive. After a while, she clears her throat and says, "Are you not going to tell me where we're going?"

"I thought I'd show you instead." I pull up in front of a waterfront hotel and a valet comes around my side of the car.

"Jonah, what's going on?"

"I know it was a pretend wedding, and that you're doing all this for Daisy, but I wanted to at least make your wedding night special. I wanted to do this for you...you deserve that."

Her throat makes a sound as she swallows, and she pinches her eyes shut. I touch her face, run my thumb along her cheek.

"Jonah. You didn't have to do this."

"Did you not hear the part where I said I wanted to?" I reach across her and open her door. "Now, come on."

"But I don't even have any clothes."

"Check the trunk. I packed your bag."

"Ohmigod, I can't believe you did this."

"Believe it."

"There had better be panties in my bag."

I laugh as I get out of the car and pop the trunk before I hand the keys to the valet. "We won't be needing them tonight. We probably won't even leave our room," I say, and Quinn's face turns red. I grab our bag from the truck, and she shakes her head.

"How did you do this without me knowing?"

I wink at her. "I have my ways."

"Oh, I know that."

I go to the counter to check us in, and Quinn twirls around, taking in the opulence of the place. Once registered, I take her hand in mine and we head to the elevator, to our honeymoon suite. We get off on the top floor, and I lead her to the door. She stands back, and I open it, but when she tries to enter, I stop her.

"Aren't I supposed to carry you over the threshold?"

She whacks me. "Cut it out."

"I'm serious," I say, and scoop her up. She yelps, then laughs as I carry her into the room.

"This place is gorgeous, Jonah. I didn't need all this."

"You deserve it though." I carry her to the window, and her eyes widen at the view of the harbor."

"What a spectacular view," she says.

"It is, but it's not what I'm interested in looking at right now."

She slowly turns my way, and there's heat in her eyes when they meet mine.

"Me neither," she says quietly, and puts her lips on mine.

I kiss her, deeply, passionately, and no matter how many times I've had this women in my bed, it will never be enough.

I carry her into the bedroom, and there's a bottle of champagne chilling and a tray of strawberries. Rose petals have been spread across the bed.

"Jonah, did you arrange for all this?"

"Yeah," I say, and set her down. "Do you like it?"

"Do you even have to ask?"

I grin at her, wanting to give her the damn world if I could. "Champagne?"

"Please."

She reaches around me, her body touching mine, teasing me viciously, as she grabs a strawberry and pops it into her mouth. "Mmm," she says, and my dick swells.

"Into strawberries, are you?" I ask.

"Mmm," she moans again as I pour the champagne and hand her a glass. We clink glasses and both take a sip. Her eyes go wide.

"This is so good."

I set my glass down and grab a strawberry. I run it over her lips then slide it into her mouth. "Just so you know, I'm into strawberries, too."

"Oh, really. Exactly how are you into them?"

"Why don't you undress for me, and I'll show you."

She smiles at me, and I step back, my eyes on her body. She takes another sip of champagne, runs her tongue over her bottom lip and sets her drink down. Her hand goes to the buttons lining her sundress, and she slowly, painfully, begins to release them.

"You're killing me, Quinn."

She tugs her bottom lip with her teeth. "I know."

I fold my arms. "Keep it up and I'll tear that dress off you."

Her chest heaves. "But this is one of my favorite dresses. It's not replaceable."

"Then you better hurry the fuck up."

Her fingers work faster, and once they're all undone, she shrugs from the dress. Fireworks go off inside my brain when she stands before me in a sexy white lace bra and matching panties.

"Did you wear these under your wedding dress?" I ask. She nods. "You wore them for me, then?"

"Yes."

"You're pretty good to me, Quinn," I say, and reach over my head to tug off my shirt. Her eyes go to my chest and she makes that sexy moan again. Fuck, man, I love the way she looks at me. "Like what you see, wife?"

Her head snaps up. "Jonah, don't call me that."

I step into her, capture her chin with my hand, and my lips come down over hers. I kiss her. Hard. Letting her know how hungry I am for her, what she means to me. I break the kiss and we're both breathless, gasping for breath.

"We just exchanged vows. Pretend or not, you're my wife, and I'm going to fuck you on this bed, consummate this marriage...okay?"

"Okay, husband," she says, and my chest puffs up as her hands snake out, pop the button on my shorts. She releases the zipper and shoves my shorts down. Her hand goes to my hard cock, and she strokes it gently.

"Fuck that feels good."

I put my hands on her face, push her hair back and revel in the hunger dancing in her eyes. She may have taken my name for Daisy's sake, but there is no denying that she wants me in her bed.

If only I could convince her to want me out of it, too.

"You're beautiful, Quinn. When I saw you in that wedding dress..." I shake my head, my mind going back to this afternoon. "I just couldn't believe how lucky I was."

"You looked so handsome, Jonah. I was the envy of every woman who saw us walk into city hall today."

I reach around her, and unhook her bra. It falls to the floor and I drop to my knees to remove her panties. Once I have her naked, I stand and press my lips to hers. I turn, taking her with me, until the backs of her knees hit the bed. My mouth never leaves hers as I give her a little nudge, until she's sitting. Her hands grip my hair and hold tight. Our lips part, and I go to my knees, and take one of her pink nipples into my mouth and suck.

"Oh, Jonah," she whispers, and I swear to Christ hearing her moan my name like that fucks me over in ways that almost frighten me. After having her in my bed numerous times, my need for her has grown, not diminished.

I suck harder, and inch back until her nipple pops from my mouth. She visibly quakes, and the small smile on her mouth urges me on. I lap at her other nipple, until it's red and swollen and marked by my mouth. Then I go back on my heels and grab a strawberry.

"Oh," she says, when I put it between my teeth and take a bite. Juice bursts in my mouth, and I take the berry and rub it over her taut nipples. She quivers at the coldness as I get them wet, then close my mouth over them in turn, offering her heat.

"I love the way you're into strawberries," she murmurs.

I chuckle against her nipple, and squeeze the berry until juice is running over her stomach. "Lay back for me," I say, and she lets herself fall, her arms going wide, her body completely offered up to me. My want for this woman is off the charts.

Here I told her I was going to ruin her, but the truth was, she's ruined me—for any other woman.

I hold the squashed berry over her mouth. "Open," I say, and place it on her tongue. She moans her approval, and I press my hands to the bed on either side of her body and run my tongue along her flesh. Her hips come off the bed as I lick the sweet strawberry juice from her quivering body.

"Jonah," she whispers, her legs automatically widening for me.

"You want my mouth here?" I say, and adjust until I'm balancing on one hand, the other going between her legs. I touch her lightly, play with her clit, and she moans and moves beneath my fingers.

"Yes, please," she says, and I chuckle. I love this uninhibited woman who has no trouble giving or taking in the bedroom. I kiss a path lower, and when her sweet perfumed scent of arousal hits me, I know I've found heaven, and it's sweeter than any strawberry.

I drop to my knees again and bury my mouth between her legs. As she cries out my name, I suck her clit into my mouth, swirl my tongue over it. She gasps and grabs at me, a desperate sort of need in her eager hands.

Knowing just how to please her, I insert one finger into her core, and find that hot bundle of nerves that drives her crazy. I stroke deeply, and her muscles tug me in as they clamp tight around me. Jesus, I'll never tire of pleasuring her this way, especially when she makes such sexy noises, letting me know just how much she loves it.

I keep my finger inside her and reluctantly tear my mouth from her clit. Right now, I need to see the pleasure on her face. Her hips come off the bed, and I nearly lose it. The sight of her like this, all warm and wanting as she lets me do things to her body, is a total mind fuck. Quinn unleashed. I fucking love it.

"Jesus, you are so sexy."

She squirms and her beautiful breasts jiggle. For a moment I think about putting my mouth back on them, but burying my face between her legs again wins out. I suck on her, eat at her like a man starved. Jesus, it's hard to keep it together with this kind of need tearing through me. I quickly remind myself to slow down. This is Quinn. A woman I'm in love with.

A woman I'm pretty sure I've been in love with my entire fucking life.

I push another finger inside for a snug fit, and every muscle in her body tightens. "I love when you come for me," I say from deep between her legs. My words push her over the edge and the next thing I know, she's coming and coming into my mouth. I drink her in, but no matter how many times I release the dam, my thirst for her will never be quenched.

"Jonah," she pants, and my cock throbs, urging me to get inside, and fast. When she stops trembling, I grab a condom from the bag I packed and slide it on.

"But I want you in my mouth," she pouts as she sits up.

"No time for that," I say, and position myself in the middle of the bed. "I need you to ride me, Quinn." Her eyes light up, obviously loving that idea, too. "I want to see my wife's face when she comes all over my cock."

I hold her arm to balance her as she tosses one leg over me and straddles my body. She cups her breasts, plays with her nipples, and I groan. "Such a boob man," she teases.

"When it comes to you, I am. Your breasts are beautiful. Everything about you is beautiful."

She shies away at that, and I touch her face.

"Hey, I'm serious."

Instead of responding, she reaches beneath her and grips my cock. "I need you inside me, Jonah," she says as she positions me at her entrance.

She lowers herself onto me, and as I sink into her body, my brain shuts down. Nothing but pleasure, for the things she does to me occupy my brain. Her hips move, rotate, massage my cock, and I clench my teeth. I grip her hips and lift her up and down, and her head falls to the side as she rides me.

"Quinn, look at me," I whisper.

Her eyes open and meet mine—and something deep and profound passes between husband and wife, something there is no coming back from.

"Quinn," I whisper.

"Jonah," she says in response, and I pray to fuck I'm not the only one invested in us right now.

Our bodies move, become one as he we make love, and our eyes never lose contact. I keep my hands on her, and she holds my arms as we work in tandem to bring each other pleasure. I lift my hips, power into her, and her clit rubs against my body with each downward movement. Her eyes dim, her lids close slightly, and she releases the softest, sexiest moan as she lets go, her cum hot on my cock.

"Yeah," I say, as sensations center in my groin, and unable to hold out any longer, I release inside her. Her eyes open a bit more and the soft smile on her face curls around my heart. It's strange, but sex with her is different this time, better now that she's my wife.

Sated, she falls over me, and I smooth my hand down her damp back, hold her close, never, ever wanting to let her go. If I told her that, would she believe me?

Would she stay on as Daisy's mother?

My wife?

Or would she run in the other direction, because a ready-made family is the last thing that she wants?

QUINN

"You got married?! To this...this...whore?"

Whore?

Oh, no she didn't!

I'm about to throat punch Shari, but Jonah puts his hand on my arm to stop me.

Honest to God, I hadn't expected this today, not after the wonderful night Jonah and I had in the honeymoon suite. We'd only just gotten home and put Daisy to bed for her nap, when Shari showed up at the door, screaming and ranting and calling me names.

I glare at her. I'm angry—not at the name calling, that I can handle. I'm angry that she didn't list Jonah as the father, that Zander had to run around to get the name of the doctor, that she left no instructions for Jonah, and neglected to tell him about her shots.

"Don't you *ever* call her that."

Jonah's voice holds a level of warning that frightens even me. Shari, however, doesn't seem fazed.

"Hand Daisy over," she demands.

"No. I'm going for custody, Shari. You disappear, show up here drunk, and then threaten me, call my wife names?"

She looks at Jonah—then laughs in his face. A chilling laugh that prowls through my blood and sets off alarm bells. Why is she laughing like she knows something we don't? My stomach sours and bile punches into my throat. Oh, this isn't good. This isn't good at all.

"Hand her over, Jonah! She's not even yours."

Jonah stands there, his entire body stiff, then he falters backward, like he'd just been sucker punched. I suppose he has been. We both have been. I put my arms around him, to help absorb the shock as my own body begins to shake almost uncontrollably.

"You're lying," he finally says through clenched teeth.

Shari plants one hand on her hip and inches her chin up. "No, I'm not."

As if refusing to believe any of this, he shoots back with, "Then why did you tell me she was mine, and drop her off here to bond with me?" He puts his hand on his stomach, like he's about to vomit, too.

"Not only are you a big fucking deal now, Jonah, when I found out I was pregnant, Zander was in love with Liz. He wasn't going to marry me, and Daisy and I need to be taken care of. But now..." She throws a disgusted look my way. "Her."

Jonah grips the back of his neck, like his head is about to split in two. His eyes are wide, frightened, and it takes me back to the day Zander called me to help and I showed up here, Jonah nursing a hangover.

"Jesus, Shari, tell me you're lying. Tell me Daisy is mine."

"She's not." Her gaze leaves Jonah and goes to me, and I plant my feet, ready to shove her out the door if need be. "Why do you think she has *your* eyes?"

"Oh. My. Fuck," I say, and sink onto the bottom step of the staircase.

Jonah drops down next to me, and I'm guessing his legs are as weak as mine as the pieces fall in to place.

"Daisy is Zander's?" I blurt out.

"Jesus, Shari, what the hell is wrong with you? Why would you do this? Fuck, I knew the condom didn't break that night, and Daisy is almost a month younger than you led me to believe." He shakes his head. "You were with Zander after me?"

As Jonah works out the details, I grab my phone and call Zander. When he answers, I tell him to get here right away. I hang on to Jonah, my heart pounding in my ears, disorienting me as I take all this in.

Shari snarls at him, "Get a paternity test done, Jonah. I'll be by tomorrow to collect my daughter. Have her ready."

With that, Shari leaves, and Jonah and I stare at each other, neither speaking, barely breathing as we sort through this turn of events. Twenty minutes later we're both still on the steps, unmoving, the front door still wide open after Shari's departure.

Zander comes through it, and when he sees us, his entire body stiffens. "What?" he asks and glances up the stairs, panic on his face. "Is Daisy okay?"

I nod, and push to shaky feet. Jonah stands with me.

"Zander," I begin. How do I tell my brother he's Daisy's father? "Let's sit."

We all move into the living room, and Zander leans forward, braces his elbows on his knees. "Does someone want to tell me what's going on? You both look like you've seen a ghost."

"Daisy..." Jonah begins. "She's not mine."

"What the fuck?"

"She's yours," he says quietly, like he's trying to soften the blow.

Zander stares at us, like we're playing a joke on him, then he pinches his eyes shut. "Jesus," is all he says.

"We'll get the tests done," I say. "To be sure this time."

"Daisy's *mine*? I'm her...father," he says, like he's trying the word on for size.

"Yeah, Shari just left, and we took Daisy to the doctor yesterday. She's younger than Shari led me to believe."

"She was trying to trap him, Zander. Don't let her do that to you," I say.

"I'm a father," he says again.

Jonah nods. "Looks like *I'm* the uncle."

Zander shakes his head. "Could this be any more fucked up?"

Jonah leans forward, grips his knees. "Dad will help with the custody papers. Anything you need. I don't think Shari really wants her, she just wants to use her as a bargaining chip."

"How am I going to take care of a child if I'm on the road? Christ, Jonah, training starts next week in Seattle."

"I'll help you," I say quickly. "Daisy is my niece. When I finally get my own center, I can take her to work with me every day."

"Then we're getting you that center sooner rather than later," Zander says.

"Zander—" I begin. He's always trying to pay my way, but I don't feel right about that.

"Damn right you are," Jonah says, and looks around his mansion. "We can convert half *this* place into a center for you. I've been thinking about that for a while now, anyway."

I sit there, flabbergasted, as the two guys I love with all my heart start discussing the details of my new daycare center. I hold my hands up to stop them.

"Hello. I'm right here. Don't you think I should have a say in this?"

Jonah reaches for my hand. "When you decided to help me—or rather, Daisy—I told you I'd make it worth your while. Let me do this for you," he says.

I take a long moment to think about it. Think about what is best for everyone. I want to help raise Daisy, and help my brother, give him security when he's away, so I swallow my pride and say, "How about this. I found this really great space in the city, I just need first and last months' rent. If you can loan it to me, then—"

"It's not a loan if I'm your husband, Quinn. You don't have to pay it back."

As soon as the words leave his mouth, my heart falls into my stomach. Now that the baby isn't is, there's no need for us to keep pretending.

Zander must sense my unease. He stands and says, "I'm going to go talk to your father, Jonah. If I really am Daisy's father, I need to get a plan in place."

"Zander," I say, and stand up, taking his hand in mine. "You okay?"

He thinks about it for a moment. "I love that little girl as much as you guys do. I eventually wanted kids, it just happened sooner rather than later. And I know I'm not alone in this. I have a great support system. Speaking of that, will you guys help me get my place set up for her, get a nanny right way?"

"Of course," I say, having never loved my brother more.

"How about I have all her things brought to your place? Maybe Quinn and I can stay the week with her, until she gets used to it."

"What about Shari?" Zander asks.

"We'll deal with her in the courts. If she really wanted Daisy, she would have taken her today."

I give Zander a hug and, after he leaves, I turn to Jonah. He's running his hand through his hair. What Shari did was so not fair to this man but now—now that Daisy isn't his—where does that leave us?

Oh, how I wanted this marriage to be real, to be a mother to that child. But deep down, Jonah's first love is hockey, a free lifestyle, and I can't compete with that. He stepped up because it was the right thing to do, not because he was ready to be a father or a husband.

I tug the ring off my finger and hold it out to him. His gaze narrows in on it. "I guess you should get your dad to draw up the divorce papers." I laugh, but it comes out shaky. "I think that might have been the shortest marriage in history."

He stares at me for a long time. "Is that what you want?"

Tell him, Quinn. Tell him what you really want.

But what if I do tell him I want to stay married? Would he even agree? We were playing house, right? Having fun. But what if he did agree? Would he end up resenting me, because he's not really ready for a family? In the end, resentment leads to abandonment, right?

"Yes," I finally say, not just for my sake, but for his too.

17

JONAH

It's been three long weeks since we've been training, and I can't eat, sleep, or even play hockey. I glance at my team as we all take shots on the net, but my thoughts aren't on today's practice. No, my thoughts are on Daisy...Quinn.

Shari never bothered to show up at my house to collect Daisy, and Dad says Zander has a good chance at full custody. Quinn hired the best nanny, and is staying at Zander's house to make the transition easier for everyone. She's also working hard to get her own center ready, so Daisy can be with family every day. My buddy Zander certainly stepped up to the plate, and I know he's going to be an amazing father to the little girl we all love.

But goddammit, if I can't be Daisy's father, I at least want to be her uncle for real. There is only one way for that to happen, but Quinn handed me the ring back, saying it was what she wanted. The fucking divorce papers are in my bag, but I've yet to sign them. I don't *want* to sign them.

I'm in love with my best friend's kid sister.

Using my own body-checking moves against me, someone

hits me from behind, and I slam into the boards with a thud. I turn around, ready to fight whoever did that, but when I find Zander standing there, shaking his head at me, I take off my helmet.

"What the fuck, dude?"

"Are you going to play the game or mope all fucking day?" he asks as he jabs me with his stick. Hard.

"Fuck off." I whack his stick way, in no mood to talk. "I'm not moping."

He laughs. "Yeah, you fucking are."

"I've just...got things on my mind," I say and look around, catch our coach watching us. Man, I need to get my shit together before he benches me.

"Like what things? My sister? The divorce papers?"

"Yeah, exactly." I'm about to skate away, but he reaches out and stops me.

"If you don't want to sign them, Jonah, then go do something about it."

I stiffen, and my heart jumps into my throat. "What are you talking about?" I study his face, take in his amused expression. He wouldn't be amused if he knew what I'd been doing with his sister, right?

Zander skates around me, giving me a good push from behind, and I jerk forward. "Jesus Christ, asshole. How stupid do you think I am?"

Fuck man, he knows. "Ah..." Zander is far from stupid. Why did I ever think I could keep something from him?

He stops in front of me, shakes off his gloves, and I brace myself, waiting for a fist to the face. But it doesn't come. Instead, he puts his hand on my shoulder. "Look. You love her. She loves you. I've stayed quiet long enough, waiting for you two to work it out. But clearly you're both too afraid to make the first move."

My stomach coils. Jesus, is he going to hate me? "How long have you known?"

"That day I showed up unannounced and Quinn was in your bed."

"Shit."

He rolls his eyes. "After that, everyone knew, Jonah."

"Everyone?" I take a deep breath and let it out slowly. "Zander, it just...sort of happened."

"Bullshit."

Great, here it comes. Not only did I lose the girl I'm fucking crazy about, now I'm going to lose my best friend, too.

"It's not—"

"Give me a fucking break. You've been crazy about Quinn for as long as I can remember. It just took the right circumstances for you to finally do something about it."

"Is this where you kick my ass?"

He laughs. "I'm a lover, not a fighter, Jonah. You're the fighter, always had my back."

It's true, I am a fighter. I fight for what I want.

So why the hell aren't I fighting for Quinn?

Because you're not what she wants, dude.

He goes serious, all humor gone from his face. "Quinn needs a good guy in her life."

"You think I'm that guy?" This is all coming at me so fast, my head starts spinning. Here I thought Zander would kill me, yet he's encouraging me to go for his sister. "Wait, you're not going to kick my ass?"

"I should." He taps his head. "For being so thick up here."

"What are you talking about?"

"Did you ever stop to wonder why your mother and father suggested the two of you get married in the first place?"

"To make it look better to the courts."

He gives a slow whistle. "Man, you've taken one too many hits to the head."

I toy with my stick and think about that. Everyone knew how I felt about Quinn? How she felt about me? My parents were...matchmaking? "Wait, you think Quinn loves me?"

He laughs. "Yeah, she fucking does."

I skate backward, then push off the boards, my heart crashing against my chest. "She gave the ring back."

"Why do you suppose she did that?" Zander arches a brow.

"Because she doesn't want a family."

"Yeah, definitely one too many hits to the head," he says. "Look, you know my sister as well as I do. She's afraid, Jonah. She's afraid that one day you'll decide you love hockey more than her, and abandon her. We all have our own demons, pal."

"Fuck, Zander." I rub the back of my neck. I worked my ass off to get where I am today. It's all I ever wanted—but I've grown up a lot in the last couple months, and my priorities shifted, big time. I love Quinn, want to have a family with her. But how can I get her to believe me, show her that she's the most important thing in the world to me? That I'm not going to abandon her—ever.

I glance at Zander as an idea grows, takes shape in my mind.

"There you go," Zander says like he can read my thoughts. He skates off, and I catch sight of Coach again, who's glaring at me. I skate toward him with single-minded determination, about to do something the Body Checker wouldn't have dreamed of doing a couple months ago.

Here goes nothing.

18
QUINN

I wave the last child off and shut the door. I lean against it and look around the daycare. Thanks to my brother and his best friend, the man I'm in love with, soon enough I'll have my own place, set my own schedule. I'm currently having the space I recently leased renovated, to get it up to code, and in a month or so my dream of running my own place will come true, and I can have Daisy with me every day.

So if my one and only dream is about to be realized, why the hell am I so miserable?

"Hey, want to go out and get a drink?" Tina asks. For the last couple weeks she's been close to my side, trying to help me move on, put the whole pretend marriage behind me.

I look at the clock. "Sure, why not," I say. What else am I going to do on a Friday night? Go home and cry myself to sleep? Daisy is in good hands, and I'll see her later, so I may as well go out.

"Maybe we can find you a man," she says and nudges me playfully.

Ugh. Truthfully, how can I ever be with another man after Jonah? The things we did, the way he made me feel. Maybe I should have just come right out and told him I wanted forever. I was too much of a chicken shit, which is so unlike me. But it was better to let him go now, than him walking away later.

"Want to talk about it?" Tina asks when I don't make a move to go.

"Not really."

"If you love him, you need to tell him."

"Yeah but—"

She holds her hand up. "No buts, Quinn. From everything you told me, Daisy changed that man, and I'm guessing he's as broken up about all of this as you are."

"He never wanted a family, Tina."

She grins at me. "What's that saying. Talk about the pot calling the kettle black."

"Yeah, but..." I pause to think about that. I swore up and down that I didn't want a family of my own. But that all changed when I started playing house with Jonah. My mind rewinds to the way he protected Daisy, the way he protected me from Shari. What was that he once said, *I protect those I care about.*

"Come to think of it, he said he could want a family if the right woman came along," I say.

"Don't you think you're that right woman?"

Is it possible that he might want the same things I do? That he didn't voice it because I'd blatantly told him I didn't want a family, that we needed to keep our relationship a secret because I didn't want people to get the wrong idea? Was he protecting me because he cares about me, maybe even loves me?

If so, pushing him away like that, assuming he'd let no one

or nothing stand in the way of his hockey, must have made him feel pretty shallow.

Have I made a horrible mistake?

"Oh, God, Tina, what have I done?" I ask, and put my hands over my face.

"It's not too late, you know."

"He's on the road. I really don't want to run after him, tell him how I feel when he's practicing."

Just then, a knock comes on the door, and I push off it. I check my watch again. "Maybe one of the kids forgot something."

I open the door—and when I see who's standing on the other side, my knees give.

"Hey," Jonah says, as he wraps his arms around me. "You okay?"

"I'm okay," I say, breathless and lightheaded.

He looks past my shoulder. "Hi, Tina," he says.

"Jonah," Tina says and backs up. "I'll just go tidy up."

"What are you doing here?" I ask. "Aren't you supposed to be at practice?"

"Yeah, I am. Coach wasn't too happy with me either, but I had to come back. There's something you need to see."

I frown, perplexed. "What are you talking about?"

"Can you come with me? I need to show you something."

I nod my head. "Yeah, okay. I guess." I turn and find Tina picking up blocks and putting them away. "Tina, would you mind if I took off?"

"Go," she says. "I got this."

Jonah doesn't touch me or even stand too close as we walk to his car. He does, however, walk me to my side, and close the door once I'm inside. My heart is racing just about as fast as my brain. What does Jonah want to show me? I'm not sure what it is, but it's obviously more important than his hockey practice.

"How have you been?" he asks as he pulls into traffic.

I look at him, take in the rumpled state of his clothes, his hair. Has he not been sleeping? I know *I* sure as hell haven't been. As I look him over, I want to tell him how I feel, but there is a part of me that holds back. Jonah is upset about something.

"Good," I say.

"Daisy?"

"She's adjusting well. She's such a happy little girl. I can't wait to get my own center open so I can have her with me all day. I've already hired staff and given my resignation at the daycare." *Okay, Quinn stop rambling already.* "How have you been?" I ask.

"Not that great."

"I'm sorry. Anything from Shari?" I ask, even though I now she's gone MIA again. Zander texts me every day asking about his daughter. If he'd heard from Shari, he would have let me know.

He shakes his head no, and I sit back and fold my hands, waiting to see what it is he needs to show me. A half hour later, he pulls up to his mansion, and I frown.

"Why are we here?"

"Come on."

He slides from the car, comes around my side and holds his hand out. Little currents of electricity sizzle though me when our fingers touch. My God, the chemistry between us hasn't diminished one little bit. Jonah sucks in a breath, clearly feeling it, too.

He guides me up the walkway and leads me into the house. I look around his place. "What?" I ask.

"Upstairs," he says.

"Jonah, what's going on?"

"Trust me," he says quietly.

"I...okay."

He puts his hand on the small of my back and leads me upstairs. He stops outside Daisy's old bedroom.

He gives me a little nudge. "Go on in."

I step into the room, expecting it to be empty. We'd brought all of Daisy's things to Zander's house. But when I flick the light on, the room is all set up again.

Wait, what is going on? Paternity tests proved Zander was the dad. Is Shari up to something?

"Jonah?"

"Follow me?"

He guides me down the hall to another bedroom, and he opens the door. This room is decorated in blue...and my heart jumps into my throat. When the hell did he do this? He's been on the road, hasn't he? But more importantly, what the hell is he trying to tell me?

Before I can ask, he tugs on my hand and leads me to another room. This one is decorated in a soft yellow, very gender neutral.

I spin and face him, take in the warm way he's looking at me.

"Jonah, how many kids do you have?" I blurt out.

The corner of his mouth turns up, making him look so sexy my thighs quiver. "I don't have any kids, Quinn."

"Then why the hell do you have three bedrooms decorated?"

"Because I wanted to show you..."

"Show me what?"

I hold my breath, hoping he's telling me what I think he's trying to. His big hand slides around my waist and he pulls me close. My God, it feels so good to be held my him.

"Here's the thing, Quinn. I'm a mess. I can't eat. I can't sleep. I can't even play hockey."

"So what does—"

He puts his finger on my lips to stop me. "I've learned so much about myself in the last couple months."

"What have you learned?" I ask, my heart wobbling in my chest.

"Hockey is important to me, very important...but it's not the most important thing in the world."

"No?"

"No—you're far more important," he says, and my heart nearly explodes with all the love I have for him. "Without you, nothing else matters."

As I look into his eyes, I see pure honesty. My brother was right, he's always been a good guy, but he's grown so much in the last few months. He looks past my shoulder into the baby's room. "I wanted to show you what you meant to me. These rooms, they're for our future."

"Jonah—"

"This is the part where I'd ask you to marry me, but you're already my wife."

"No I'm not, I signed the papers."

He pulls something from his back pocket and hands it to me. It's our divorce papers, and they're missing his signature.

"I want to be married to you, Quinn. For real. Not because of Shari, or Daisy, or the courts, but because I love you. I wanted this to be real the first time around, but you said you didn't want a family, and I was trying to respect that."

Tears spill from my eyes. "I do want this, Jonah. I love you, too. I just... I was afraid."

He hugs me tighter, and his thumb brushes over my cheek. "I know, but I'm not like your mother, Quinn. I walked away from hockey practice and I'll likely be benched the first few games because of it. But I did it to prove to you that you are way more important."

My heart swells, knowing he did this all for me.

He brushes his lips over mine. "If you want to know the truth, I've been in love with you since you were sixteen."

My eyes go wide. "You're kidding me?"

He shakes his head. "Nope, but Zander..."

"I kind of figured he knew." I look him over. "And you're still in one piece?"

He laughs. "He's a lover, not a fighter, and he's happy for us."

I go up on my toes and press my lips to his. He holds me to him, and when I break the kiss, I say, "I have a confession, too."

"Yeah?"

"I've been in love with you for a very long time, Jonah. I only acted like I hated you because you treated me like one of the guys."

"Had to. Bro code and all."

I roll my eyes at him but I get it. "You should probably know, I spent days making hearts in my journals, putting 'Quinn loves Jonah' inside them."

He laughs hard. "Are you kidding me?"

I shake my head and laugh with him. "I'll show you someday."

"Quinn?"

"Yeah?"

He pulls a ring from his back pocket. "Will you still be my wife?" he asks.

"Yes!" I say, and let loose a big squeal when he picks me up and spins me around.

"Will you help me fill these rooms with kids? I want a big-ass family."

"So do I," I say, and he picks me up.

"What are you doing?"

"Getting started."

"On what?"

"Filling these rooms, of course."

"Shouldn't the Body Checker be in Seattle, doing what he does best."

"Really, Quinn, after all the time you spent in my bed, you still think hockey is what I do best?"

"Well no...not really," I say, my heart so full of love, and my body so alive for this man to take me again, I can barely think straight.

He carries me to his room, sets me on the bed and stands back. "Undress now," he demands in a soft command, as his eyes rake over me. "The Body Checker has a body to check out."

I laugh at that, and reach for the small buttons on my shirt.

The need making his eyes go dark, sends heat through my body. "Uh, are you fond of that shirt?" he asks.

I grin. "Not really," I say.

He drops to his knees before me, grips the shirt and tears it wide open. I gasp, and his mouth goes to body. "That's better, wife," he says between kisses.

My heart soars, loving how he calls me that. "I'm going to go through a whole wardrobe with you, aren't I?"

"Yes, and I'll buy you a new one with no goddam small buttons." His mouth leaves my flesh, and he stands, runs his tongue runs along my neck.

"You don't have—" I begin, but when he tugs the cup of my bra down and closes his mouth over my nipple, all thoughts fade except for how much I love this man, and how I now have everything I've ever wanted, but never thought I could have. He draws my nipple in, and I let loose a soft moan that pulls a growl from him.

"Such a boob man," I tease.

"That's not all I'm into," he says, his voice vibrating through me.

"I know," I whisper, and rake my hands through his hair. "And now you have a lifetime to show me."

"Some of those things might be weird."

I laugh at that. "I wouldn't expect anything less."

AFTERWORD

Thank You!

Thank you so much for reading The Body Checker, book three in my Players on Ice series. I hope you enjoyed the story as much as I loved writing it. Be sure to check The Playmaker, and The Stick Handler. Please read on for an excerpt of Single Dad Next Door.

Interested in leaving a review? Please do! Reviews help readers connect with books that work for them. I appreciate all reviews, whether positive or negative.

Happy Reading,
   Cathryn

SINGLE DAD NEXT DOOR

When my bedroom door flies open and crashes hard against the paint-chipped wall, I groan. "Go away," I say, my voice muffled by my pillow. Not that my roommates will listen, even if they can hear me. Heck, I could scream at the top of my lungs and it wouldn't faze them, much less send them running back to their rooms —not when the view outside my window is that *hot*.

Seriously though, sharing a house with four college freshmans is not my idea of a good time, not when I'm a senior and working my ass off to get into law school. But when I left NYU two months before the start of my fourth year and transferred to Penn State at the last minute, this place was all I could find—and afford. Ultimately, Penn State is where I want to do my law degree after undergrad. I just ended up here sooner, rather than later.

Someone tugs at my pillow and I open one eye to see Becca hovering over me. "Come on, Rach, he just took his shirt off," she says. "You're going to want to see this."

Why oh why did my room have to come with the best view of the hot neighbor's driveway?

"Thank God for this heat wave." Sylvie, roommate number two, fans her face with her hand.

I groan and curl up into the fetal position. I just want one more minute in bed without every member of the house in my room. "I. Don't. Care." Well, that might be a lie. I like looking at the eye candy next door as well as they do, but after putting in a late night at Pizza Villa—I seriously have to find a new job—I need all the sleep I can get before class.

"Jesus, would you look at him," Becca says, her voice a breathy whisper as she peers out the window. "Talk about slurpalicious. I could seriously lick that from head to toe, and back up again."

"Leave," I say on a yawn.

Ignoring me, Sylvie squeals. "He's going back into his garage. Damned if he doesn't look as good going as he does coming."

"But I'd rather see him...*coming*," Becca says, and they start giggling.

"Seriously. Are you both twelve?"

"Shh, he's back," Becca says and swats her hand at me, like I'm an annoying fly that needs to be shooed away.

I shift on my bed, not to get a better look outside my window. No, moving has absolutely nothing at all to do with the shirtless mechanic turning my roommates into dim-witted moths. The *only* reason I'm getting up is to herd these girls from my room, and if I happen to get a glimpse of the hot, tattooed, badass daddy next door, well...then so be it.

I rub the blur from my eyes and toss my pillow at them. "Get away from my window, before he thinks it's me." They don't need to know that the hottie's bedroom window is also across from mine, and that late one night, he caught me staring into his room as he walked around in nothing but boxer shorts. Heck, if they knew that, they'd camp out for the rest of the school year, and that was so not happening.

"Ohmigod!" Sylvie leaps back. "I think he just saw me." She puts her hand over her mouth and starts to giggle. Footsteps pound down the hall, announcing the arrival of my other two roommates. I shake my head as they come bursting in.

Kill. Me. Now.

"Is he out there?" Val asks, her big blue eyes wide and hopeful.

"Yeah, but he saw me looking," Sylvie says. Despite that, she edges back around to sneak another look. Megan hurries across the room, and goes up on her toes to peer over Sylvie's shoulder, trying to catch a glimpse without getting caught.

"Do you really think he killed someone?" Megan asks.

"That's the rumor," Val protests, though her tone holds uncertain convictions.

"Then why isn't he in jail?"

"Maybe it was self-defense."

"He's such a badass."

"He's good with his little girl, though."

"Bad Boy Daddy, now that's hot."

"Do you think he'd spank me if I was bad?"

Unable to put up with their incessant chatter and giggles any longer, I point my finger toward the door. "Out. Now."

A chorus of grumbles ensues as they all sullenly walk to my door. Christ, I'm getting that lock fixed, even if I have to eat ramen noodles for the next month.

"God, you're such a grouch in the morning." Becca shoots me a wounded look over her shoulder.

"Doesn't even have to be the morning," Val adds with a hair toss.

"You need to get your nose out of a book once in a while," Megan says.

"What she needs is to get laid," Sylvie informs them all, but her solution to pretty much everything is sex. Problem is, this time Megan is nodding her head in sad agreement as she follows Sylvia out the door.

"I can hear you," I shout after them. I shake my head and my mussed hair falls over my shoulders. "I'm still right here." As I stand there, dressed only in my tank top and underwear, a warm breeze blows in and slides over my skin, a late reminder that I'd opened my window last night before crawling into bed exhausted. Great. Not only could the hot guy working on his car see my roommates drooling over him, he could *hear* them as well. *And* they just announced that I needed to get laid. How freaking mortifying. I stomp across the room and yell down the hall, "And don't bother to close my door on your way out." As usual my sarcasm is ignored.

I give the door a good slam, which helps improve my mood a little. With a deep breath, I turn around, not to see my hot neighbor, but to close my window. No way do I want him hearing anything else that goes on inside this place, or get the wrong idea that I might want him. I don't. Not in a million years.

I'm completely off guys, trying to keep a low profile. After my ex-boyfriend turned violent and abusive, threatening to kill me if I went to the police, I snuck away under the cover of darkness and put several states between us. His was big and hard like my neighbor, his muscles born from rough carpentry work. Last year, when he came to do repairs on the house I was sharing with friends, I was flattered that I was the object of his attention. At first he was doting and attentive, but as time went by, he became possessive and controlling, and I came to find out later, he'd had other charges against him from numerous other women.

Jesus, why am I such a bad judge of character when it comes to men. Oh, probably because my only role model had been a mean-assed, alcoholic father who drove my beautiful, caring mom to an early grave and me out of the house the second I turned eighteen.

If I try hard enough I can still smell the cheap perfume on his shirt when he stumbled in after a weekend-long drinking binge. God, how I hated those women he slept around with almost as much as I hated my Dad. Mom used to try to protect me from his disgusting behavior, but what hurt the most was how dragged Mom down, aging her pretty face far too early.

My heart squeezes as I think about her. She was a good woman, but was too afraid to leave. Running is hard. I get that now. Not that she really had anywhere to run. Our only other relative was my father's mother. She's still alive, living upstate Pennsylvania where my Dad was born. While she liked me well enough, when it came to Mom and Dad, she always took Dad's side. That's how it is with parents, I guess.

I lift my arms, place my hands on the frame, and lean in to give it a tug when the hottie slowly lifts his head. Our eyes meet, hold a moment too long, and I suck in a quick breath as heat zings through me—and dammit, it's not the autumn sun that has warmth pooling between my legs.

OMFG.

With a wrench clasped tightly in his right hand he stares at me, like we're in a goddamn Mexican standoff. I swallow hard, and will myself to move, but can't seem to tear my gaze away. Ah, what was that I said about dim-witted moths?

Close the window, Rachel.

While my brain struggles to call the shots, my body has other ideas. Ideas that involve staying exactly where I am and ogling the hottest guy I'd ever seen. Blue eyes, square jaw, a body I could play Plinko on, and low riding, well-worn jeans that accentuate bulges in all the right places, and holy hell, the man has a lot of right places. Want prowls through me, hitting every erogenous spot along the way.

Just shut the window already.

He shifts his stance and taps the wrench against his leg as he looks up am me. A small grin touches his mouth, and that's when I realize I'm half naked. *Please, ground, open up and swallow me.* After hearing the girls, he probably thinks I'm trying to lure him to my room, fix that dry spell I've been going through. I grip the window ledge tighter and slam it down, putting the brakes on my body's reaction, and shutting out six delicious feet of hard muscle and pure testosterone. This is so not what I need right now. Coffee. Yeah, that's what I need. Lots and lots of coffee.

I hurry to the kitchen and shove a pod into the Keurig. I pour milk into a cup and set it on the spill tray. As I wait for the coffee to percolate, I wander into the main level bathroom and glance in the mirror. I look at myself and try to imagine how I appeared through the blue-eyed mechanic's eyes. I see black smudges under tired eyes, boobs that only look big because I'm slender from work, school and lack of proper nutrition and rest. My hair is…wait… I grab a fistful of my curls and examine them closer. Oh, God, pizza sauce.

Could this day get any worse?

Christ, even if he did hear my roommates, I'm sure he'd never look twice at a girl like me—especially the way I look now. A guy like him probably goes out with women who are a little more put together, sexier. Although I have to say in the two months I've lived here, I've never seen a woman come or go from his place. Still, I'm certain a girl next door who always smells like marinara sauce and pepperoni isn't even on his radar.

Good, because I don't want to be.

The coffee machine beeps and I hurry back to the kitchen. I grab the mug to take a big sip. Heavenly. Desperate for a shower, to wash last night's work from my hair, I hurry back upstairs to my room, hot mug of coffee in hand. I check the time and grab my clothes. Giggles come from Sylvie's room across the hall as I dash into the bathroom. I turn the shower to cool, partly because it's just so hot in the house, and partly because I need to calm my overheated body down. I might be off men, especially big, scary ones like my neighbor, but my body and brain aren't working in sync this morning. Clearly my libido didn't get the memo when I left New York.

I stay under the needle-like spray longer than normal, needing an extra minute to clear my head. When the water turns cooler, I jump out, dry off, and pull on a pair of shorts and T-shirt. I towel try my hair, then tie it back into a ponytail. I forgo makeup. Not only will it melt off my face, I'm not trying to impress anyone or draw any kind of attention to myself. Once done, I grab my purse, shove my textbooks into my backpack, and head for the front door, feeling a little more alive after the coffee.

The hot morning air hits like a slap in the face and I groan. It's October for God's sake. It's supposed to be time for pumpkin spiced lattes. This is more like beach weather. Mother nature needs to get her shit together. I glance at my watch, and judging by the time—thanks to an extra-long shower—I need to get my shit together, too. This morning I'll have to take my car to school, or risk being late for class. The walk to campus is long, around forty-five minutes, but I prefer it on days like today. I need to save my gas money for the colder winter months.

Since my driveway runs parallel to my neighbor's, I keep my head down, toss my backpack into the back seat and climb into the driver's side. Thank God the hottie is out of sight and I don't have to go through the embarrassment of facing him.

I roll my window down and shove the key into the ignition. I turn it, only for the engine to make some god-awful sound and stall out. My heart races quicker. Shit. Shit. Shit. Frustrated, I give the steering wheel a thump with my fist. This can't be happening. I need this car. Need to be able to depend on it if I have to run again. I might be an old junker, but it's all I have. I can't afford a new one. Heck, I'm on such a tight budget, I can't even afford to have this one fixed.

I take a deep breath, throw up a silent prayer, and twist the key again, only for it to cough and gasp, like it's dying a slow and painful death.

No. No. No

A tap comes on the roof, and I turn to see my hot—shirtless—neighbor with his arms braced over the door of my car. He leans down, his beautiful face close to mine. "Need a hand?"

"I...uh...it's not working."

Jeez, way to state the obvious.

He grins, and when I see a cute dimple that contrasts sharply with his chiseled face, I nearly swallow my tongue.

"Yeah, I kind of got that, you know, being a mechanic and all." As he gives off a bad-boy vibe that messes with my common sense, he grabs a cloth from his back pocket, and wipes his hands before leaning into the car, his head practically in my lap.

Holy fuck!

It takes everything, and I mean *everything*, in me not to grab the back of his head and shove it between my legs. My sex practically quivers at the visual. The girls were right. I do need to get laid. I bite the inside of my cheek to stifle the moan rising in my throat.

"What...what are you doing?" I finally manage to ask, and will myself not to writhe restlessly, and show him what a needy girl I really am.

He pulls the hood release, and the front end of my car jumps. His head lifts and once again his face is close to mine.

"Popping the hood." He angles his head, and his eyes narrow. "What did you think I was doing?"

Oh, I don't know. Maybe you were taking this opportunity to go down on me.

"Popping the hood," I say quickly, and try not to think of sex. Dirty sex. Take-me-up-against-the-wall kind of sex. Not that I know anything about that. Sadly.

His laugh is rough and deep as he walks around to the front of the car, and I unbuckle quickly. My legs wobble as I climb out of the driver's seat and follow him. He's grinning when I reach him.

"What?" I ask, my voice raspy.

He touches my cracked windshield washer cap, which I happened to repair all by myself. "Duct tape?" he asks, his voice amused.

"Tools of the trade, right," I say and try not to sound as breathless as I feel. A difficult task considering I'm standing next to a half-naked man that I want to run my hands all over. I mean I've seen shirtless guys before, but come on. This guy is like a freaking viking. He leans forward to fiddle with something, and the movement shows off impressive bicep muscles. I break a sweat as his closeness sends shudders of need between my thighs. Honest to God, the man is a work of art, and all I can think of is no-strings sex—something I've never done before. But that's crazy and reckless and so not me. Truthfully, if I knew what was good for me, I'd slam the hood shut and run in the opposite direction.

I'm about to do just that when he says, "Uh, huh."

"Is...is there something wrong?" Is that my voice? Christ, I sound like I'm whacked out on painkillers.

For God's sake, get it together, girl.

He rubs the scruff on his chin, and I step back, needing a measure of distance before I actually reach out and run my hands over all his hard grooves and deep valleys.

"Plenty," he says again and checks something else. I have no clue what he's doing. I only know that he looks as hot as hell doing it. As he leans over my car, my gaze slides to his ass, committing the way his pants cup his cheeks to memory. The guy could be in a jeans commercial, or better yet, a Calvin Klein underwear ad. I'm a girl, but advertising like that would have me one-clicking the buy button.

My heart hammers as he stands again. He turns toward me, but I'm far too slow to react. His eyes are piercing, almost a deeper shade of blue when my gaze jerks to his, and I can't tell whether he's thrilled or pissed to find me checking him out.

I step closer and look over the engine. "So, what is it?" I ask, disgusted with myself. I should not be fantasizing over this man.

He clears his throat. "I think the first thing we need to do is replace the spark plugs," he answers, his voice a little hoarse.

"Yeah, that's what I was thinking," I say, my head bobbing in agreement.

That grin is back when I look at him. "You know something about cars?"

I shrug. "Sure...and duck tape."

He laughs and says, "It's not..." he shakes his head. "Never mind. So, you agree then, that something's not firing right?"

Firing? Oh, things were firing all right, and lighting up my body like a goddamn Fourth of July celebration.

Damn him.

Damn Mother Nature.

Damn dim-witted moths.

***

Jaxon:

I grab the rag from my back pocket and swipe a bead of moisture from my forehead, as the girl from the upstairs bedroom stands next to me, looking so goddamn hot in her tight AC/DC t-shirt and ripped jean shorts that her car isn't the only thing close to overheating. If I didn't love the band before, I sure as hell would now.

She might have lived next to me for two months, and numerous times I've glimpsed her moving around her bedroom with little to nothing on, but this is the first time I've been so close to her—and it's making it a little fucking hard to breathe.

Talk about fueling all my college girl fantasies.

Not only is she gorgeous, everything about her, from the swell of her cleavage, her barely-there curves, to legs that go on for miles, reminds me it's been a long-ass time since I've had a woman in my bed. It's not that women are on my *do without* list, which is sizable now that I'm the sole caregiver to a five-year-old girl. It's just that after working all day and being a full-time single parent at night, it leaves little time for anything else. That, and I have to be very careful who I let into my daughter's life. No way will I ever let anyone hurt her again.

My sexy neighbor bends over the hood to examine the car again, and my cock twitches—very well aware of how long it's been since it's been touched, too. I try not to chuckle as she tugs on some wires, acting like she knows what she's doing. A moment later, she stands and shifts from one foot to another, her nervous gaze darting from me, to the cars passing by, back to the engine.

"Will it take long?" she asks, as I resist the urge to adjust my thickening cock.

Probably not.

"Uh..." I search for my words, my hard cock interfering with my brain process.

Her eyes fly back to mine. "The car, I mean. Will it take long?" she explains, like I'd misunderstood what she'd meant the first time. I didn't. I just had my mind on other things that likely wouldn't take long, you know, because of the huge hard on I'm sporting at eight in the morning.

I check my watch. "Not long, but I won't be able to get at it for a bit."

She blinks thick lashes over the prettiest brown eyes I've ever seen. "Um…how much will it cost, do you think?"

Her breathy question has me thinking about plunging my hands through her hair and bending her over the hood so I can fulfill all my dirty college-girl fantasies. All I can think about is fucking her until her roommates hear her screams.

"Have you noticed the temperature gauge going high?"

"Yeah, when I was at the stoplight last week, I noticed that."

"Well then, it's not the spark plugs that are going to set you back. It's the radiator. It needs to be replaced."

"Oh…damn." She chews on her bottom lip and crinkles her nose. That's when her scent hits me. Peaches. Why the fuck does she have to smell like sweet peaches? My goddamn favorite fruit. "Maybe we better forget this."

She starts to back away, and I have no idea why, but I'm not ready for this conversation to be over. "Look, I can probably get you a good deal on one, cut your costs in half, and I can do the labor for free."

Jesus, what the fuck am I doing?

"I can't—"

Just then Cassie sticks her head out the upstairs window. "Daddy, I can't find my shoes."

I shade the early morning sun from my eye and my heart misses a beat the way it always does when I see my little girl. "We came in the back door last night, remember?"

"Right."

Cassie disappears and I hear my neighbor mumbling under her breath. Apparently, a broken-down car, one she can't afford to have fixed, is going to make her late for class.

I shove the rag back into my pocket and close the hood. "What time do you need to be there?"

She blinks up at me. "What?"

The lock clicks into place. "School. What time do you have to be there?"

"Thirty minutes."

"I can get you there on time." I nod toward the window my daughter just stuck her head out of. "I'll drop Cassie off, then take you."

She shakes her head fast. "I don't want to put you out like that."

Put me out? Oh, she can put me out anytime, or better yet, put out for me.

I scrub the scruff on my chin. "It's not a problem... uh...shit, I don't even know your name."

"Rachel," she says.

"Jaxon." I hold a hand out for her to shake it, and she hesitates, going back to shifting her weight from one foot to the other. Cassie does that when she has to go to the bathroom. But I don't think that's Rachel's problem. Tension vibrates from her, and I take in the almost fearful way she's staring at my hand. Why the fuck is she afraid of me? Is it the murder rap her friends were talking about, or is it something else altogether?

I eye her carefully, note the way she continually casts uneasy glances over her shoulder as she shifts. I might be on the straight and narrow now, but over the years I'd be dragged up and kicked around. I'd survived playground bullies, cruel foster parents, and poverty, so yeah, I know a girl on the run when I see one.

"Jaxon Morgan," I say and continue to hold my hand out,

and think back to the night she showed up here, with nothing but a rundown car and her belongings in a backpack. No family or friends to help. While I realize trouble is the last thing I need in my life—with the in-laws trying to prove I'm an unfit parent—I can't just turn my back on her. I'm not looking to be anyone's savior, but Christ, it's obvious this girl could use a fucking break.

"I'm not going to hurt you, Rachel." I roll one shoulder as a strange kind of protectiveness grips me. "Just offering a ride and a deal on some car work. We're neighbors after all, right?"

She shoves her hand into mine, and I give it a squeeze. "Right, sorry...I..." She exhales and gives me a smile, like she wants to start over again. "I appreciate it. Thank you."

"Can you give me a minute to get Cassie's lunch packed?"

"Sure."

"Come have a seat inside the shop. Get out of the sun while I get her ready." She snags her purse from her car, locks the doors behind her and follows me into the service bay, aka the bottom half of my house. I grab a piece of paper from behind the counter and gesture toward my cleanest chair. "Have a seat there, and fill in your contact information."

"Oh, okay. What do you need that for?"

"Just in case I run into trouble working on the car and need to run something by you." I give her a wink. "Since you know so much about fixing vehicles."

She smirks as she fishes a pen from her purse, and that's when I realize how much I like her, how easy she is to be around. Not that I know her. I don't. But I love how she shut down her roommates this morning when they were all staring at me. The only one I like watching me is her. Yeah, I caught her checking me out—and not just this morning.

Dammit, don't go there, Jaxon. Cassie needs stability, and you can't bring trouble into your life.

"I'll be right back." I dash up the stair, tug on a T-shirt

and hurry into the kitchen. I grab Cassie's empty cereal bowl and drop it into the sink. It teeters on top of the pile of dishes already stacked high. Cassie comes skipping down the hall.

She holds her sneakers up for me to see. "I found them."

I grin at her, and run my hands over her hair. "Good girl. Are you ready?"

"Yeah, but I want twisted pony, Daddy."

Twisted pony, aka top twisted pony braid. I groan inwardly. Even after watching the braiding ninjas on YouTube, my big fingers struggle to get it right. According to Cassie, we usually end up with Nightmare Moon—a reference to the villain on My Little Pony. Sometimes I swear she asks just to torture me.

"How about we just put it up into a ponytail." My mind rushes back to the no-nonsense way Rachel wears her hair. While I like that, I'd love to pull the elastic out and watch those long curls spill over my sheet. I clear my throat. Fuck man, I need to stop fantasizing about my neighbor.

"Please..." she says.

"Okay, hurry, grab the elastic and brush. I have a customer downstairs and I need to give her a drive because her car is broken down."

As Cassie dashes back down the hall, I reach for her lunch box, but it hits the pile of dishes and two plates clatter to the floor and break.

Fuck. I do not have time for this. "Cassie, don't come in here," I yell out.

I crouch down and pick up the big shards of glass and drop them into the garbage can. One cuts my finger. "Shit." I shove it into my mouth.

"Are you okay?" My head jerks up to see a breathless Rachel standing in the doorway. "Sorry, I heard a crash, and thought you might need some help." Her gaze leaves mine and takes in the state of my kitchen. Fuck, the in-laws are threatening to call child protection services. If they showed up now, I'd surely lose Cassie. But I've been so busy at work, and with Cassie starting kindergarten, I'd gotten a little behind on the housework. Then again, it's also possible I got a little lax because they've been away for the last month, vacationing in the Caribbean. Apparently, their absent daughter, and my 'unfit' parenting hasn't prevented them from jet-setting around the world.

"Excuse the mess."

"No, it's okay," she says quickly, her t-shirt shifting over her breasts as she rests a shoulder against the kitchen doorframe and folds her arms. Does she have any idea how sexy she looks standing there? "You should see my bedroom."

"I...uh...I have seen your bedroom," I say. "It's always clean and tidy."

Her eyes go wide and a blush spreads across her cheeks. "You...you've seen my room?"

"It's across from mine, hard not to, right?"

Hard being the key fucking word here. Cause yeah, that shit's happening between my legs again.

"Yeah, true. I can see yours, too. Not that I'm trying to look or anything. It's just that sometimes when I'm up late studying, you have your light on, and your blinds open, and like you said, our windows are directly across from one another." A nervous laugh catches in her throat. "I could toss you a slice of pizza. Sometimes I bring a pie home with me." As she rambles on, I take in the flush on her cheeks. Damn if she isn't sexy when flustered.

"Rachel."

She stops for a moment, takes a deep breath, and lets it out slowly. "Yeah?"

"Can you hand me the broom?" I gesture toward it, and she steps into the kitchen to hand it to me.

"I'm not like my roommates though," she starts up again. "And I want to apolog—"

"Daddy, what happened?" Cassie gasps as she pokes her head into the kitchen, her big blue eyes wide as she takes in the broken dishes. "You're bleeding." She makes a move toward me, but Rachel runs and grabs her before she can walk on the glass.

"I dropped a couple plates, and it's just a little scratch. Stay there, okay, and get your shoes on. I don't want you to get cut. And say hello to our new friend Rachel. She's the client I'm giving a drive to."

Rachel crouches down to Cassie's height, and smiles at her. "Hello, Cassie. I've seen you around but we've never really met before."

"You're Daddy's friend?"

"Yes."

Cassie crinkles her nose. "You're a girl."

"I am."

"Does the mean you're his girlfriend?"

"No, no," Rachel says quickly and explains the difference between girl friend, and girlfriend.

"You're pretty," Cassie says, and I glance up to see her holding her brush and elastics out. "Daddy was going to braid my hair and make me pretty, too."

"You don't need your hair braided to make you pretty, but how about I do it for you, since your dad has to put a bandage on his hand."

Cassie leans into Rachel. "Daddy makes Nightmare Moon."

"Nightmare Moon, what is that?"

"Her name is Princess Luna but when she's evil they call her Nightmare Moon."

"So you're saying your dad makes evil braids?"

"I can hear you," I say, but my heart is in my throat as I

see how quickly my child has taken to our neighbor. Cassie has seen her around of course, and they've waved in passing, so truthfully Rachel isn't a stranger to her. None of the college girls next door are.

Rachel giggles with Cassie, and in my heart I know how much my little girl needs a mother, one who isn't an addict and chose a life of drugs and partying over her family. I tried to help her, I really did, but in the end, she ran off with her dealer, without so much as a glance at us in the rearview mirror. I guess we weren't enough for her to get clean. Then again, I was labeled a lowlife and was never enough for anyone to stick around. But I plan to do everything in my power to be enough for Cassie. Outside of her grandparents I'm all she has.

My in-laws were always worried about me taking care of Cassie—considering my past—when they should have been worried about their own daughter. But they didn't know what was really going on behind closed doors, and I didn't want to be the one to shatter their image of their sweet Sarah, a college-educated girl from an upper-class family who veered off track. They blame me for that, but I was slowing down on the partying scene when I met her, and gave it up completely after Cassie was born.

"I think I want a ponytail, like you," Cassie says, bringing my thoughts back.

"Easy enough." Rachel holds her hand out for the brush and elastics, and Cassie hands them to her.

Rachel stands, and turns Cassie around. As she combs out my daughter's hair, I sweep up the rest of the glass, wash and bandage my finger, then grab Cassie's lunch from the fridge. I drop the food into her plastic lunchbox, and look up to find the two girls chatting quietly.

"Are you two whispering about me?" I ask

"No," they both say in unison, but from the grin on Rachel's face, I know it's a lie.

"All right, come on. Let's get you both to school."

"You go to school?" Cassie asks Rachel as we make our way downstairs and back outside.

"I do?"

"What grade are you in?"

"Well, I'm in college?"

"What's college?"

Rachel glances at me and I shake my head. "Chatty Cassie," I say.

I open the door to the back seat as Rachel grabs her backpack from her car. "In you go, kiddo."

Cassie climbs into her car-seat and buckles herself in. "Good?" I ask.

"Good?" she says and picks up her mock iPad and turns it on. As music blares, Rachel slides into the passenger seat. Once we're all buckled up, I back out of the driveway and head to Cassie's school.

Rachel casts me a glance. "You have your hands full."

I scrub my chin and flick on my signal. "Yeah. She's definitely a full-time job, but I wouldn't change it for the world." Rachel shifts restlessly beside me, and I don't miss the curiosity in her big brown eyes. "What?"

"It's not my business, but I take it her mom's not in the picture."

I stiffen and grip the steering wheel tighter, and Rachel holds her hands up, palms out. "Sorry, none of my business. I wasn't trying to pry."

"No, it's okay. I just..." I pause, not wanting to divulge too much about myself. "You're right, her mom's not in the picture. She left a couple years ago and we've not seen her since. It's just Cassie and me."

"I'm sorry, Jaxon."

"Yeah, me too," I say, and clench down on my jaw.

"I was thinking..."

I cast her a quick glance, note the way she's playing with the straps on her purse. "About?"

"That you could use a little help around your place, and with Cassie. Everyone needs a break once in a while right? You're giving me one with my car."

"What are you suggesting?"

"That maybe I could help you around the house. Cook, clean, babysit, teach you how to braid Cassie's hair," she says with a grin. "Although I hear you make a mean Nightmare Moon."

I laugh at that. "Yeah, I guess you're right. What's the going rate for something like that?" I ask. I'm not hurting for money. I have a very successful business, and have been thinking about hiring someone to help me with the house. I just haven't found the time to look more into it. That, and I don't trust too many people with my belongings—time in juvenile hall will do that to you—or with my daughter.

"Well, I was thinking, instead of money, I could spend the next couple weeks working off the repairs to the car. You're helping me, I'm helping you."

"Tit for tat?"

Shit, now I'm thinking of her tits.

"Yeah, exactly."

I mull that over as I pull up to Cassie's school. I jump out as she unbuckles herself. The second I open her door, she hops from the car and is about to take off until I bend to give her a hug and kiss. "I'll see you later, kiddo."

"Bye, Daddy. Bye, Rachel," she says and I wave to the playground monitor as Cassie runs to catch up to her friends. I slide back into the car and pull in to traffic.

"Okay, so tit for tat. I like it."

I like it a lot. Which is a real fucking problem.

"Um, just one thing you should know, Jaxon."

"What's that?"

She continues to twist the strap of her purse. "What you heard this morning...from my friends."

I shake my head and laugh. "I heard a lot from your friends."

"Yeah, but the part about—"

"Me having killed someone. For the record, I never killed anyone. Gave a few good beatings to a few bad people who deserved them, but I never murdered anyone."

Rachel nods her head. "Good to know, but I'm talking about—"

"You needing to get laid?"

ABOUT CATHRYN

New York Times and *USA today* Bestselling author, Cathryn is a wife, mom, sister, daughter, and friend. She loves dogs, sunny weather, anything chocolate (she never says no to a brownie) pizza and red wine. She has two teenagers who keep her busy with their never ending activities, and a husband who is convinced he can turn her into a mixed martial arts fan. Cathryn can never find balance in her life, is always trying to find time to go to the gym, can never keep up with emails, Facebook or Twitter and tries to write page-turning books that her readers will love.

Connect with Cathryn:
Newsletter
https://app.mailerlite.com/webforms/landing/c1f8n1
Twitter: https://twitter.com/writercatfox
Facebook:
https://www.facebook.com/AuthorCathrynFox?ref=hl
Blog: http://cathrynfox.com/blog/

Goodreads: https://www.goodreads.com/author/show/91799.Cathryn_Fox

Pinterest http://www.pinterest.com/catkalen/

ALSO BY CATHRYN FOX

Hands On
Hands On
Body Contact
Full Exposure

Dossier
Private Reserve
House Rules
Under Pressure
Big Catch

Boys of Beachville
Good at Being Bad
Igniting the Bad Boy
Bad Girl Therapy

Stone Cliff Series:
Crashing Down
Wasted Summer
Love Lessons
Wrapped Up

Eternal Pleasure Series
Instinctive

Impulsive

Indulgent

Sun Stroked Series

Seaside Seduction

Deep Desire

Private Pleasure

Captured and Claimed Series:

Yours to Take

Yours to Teach

Yours to Keep

Firefighter Heat Series

Fever

Siren

Flash Fire

Playing For Keeps Series

Slow Ride

Wild Ride

Sweet Ride

Breaking the Rules:

Hold Me Down Hard

Pin Me Up Proper

Tie Me Down Tight

Take Me Down Tender

Stand Alone Title:

Hands on with the CEO

Torn Between Two Brothers

Holiday Spirit

Unleashed

Knocking on Demon's Door

Web of Desire